GHOST STORY

by

G.V. PEARCE

Improbable
PRESS

A SHERLOCKIAN ROMANCE

First published by Improbable Press in 2020

Improbable Press is an imprint of:
Clan Destine Press
www.clandestinepress.net
PO Box 121, Bittern
Victoria 3918 Australia

National Library of Australia Cataloguing-In-Publication data:

Pearce, G.V.

Ghost Story

ISBN: 978-0-6487414-1-1 (pb)
ISBN: 978-0-6487414-2-8 (eb)

Cover © Willsin Rowe
Design & Typesetting: Clan Destine Press

Improbable Press
www.improbablepress.co.uk

With thanks to Cathy, Julian, Caitlin,
and the city of York.

Imagination is all we have,
but with that we can build anything.

CHAPTER ONE

Present Day – London to York

SHERLOCK WAS KEEPING THINGS FROM HIM.

John jolted from a dream of dark caves where sand crunched endlessly under his feet to find that the train had just pulled into Peterborough station.

The announcer, or maybe just a change in the train's vibrations, must have woken him. It hadn't been Sherlock, because he didn't seem to realise John was awake.

If he had noticed, Sherlock would probably have made some move to hide the evidence of the case he'd said he wasn't going to take.

The woman who'd been sitting opposite them since King's Cross must have gone to the restaurant car because Sherlock had covered more than half the surface of the table with papers. Poorly photocopied cuttings from Gloria Evans' diaries were mixed with pencil-sketched maps of York, all marked in Sherlock's own cryptic handwriting. Here and there a type-written page stood out from the mess, but the text was too small. Atop the detritus was a pair of professional-looking digital portraits of Gloria – one older with slate grey hair, the other gaunt with her hair shaved close to her head. Sherlock must have commissioned someone to age up one of the photographs they'd found in Gloria's flat.

Staring at the friendly, slightly-pixelated smile, John couldn't help but feel a little betrayed. All this work must have taken some time, but Sherlock hadn't told him about any of it.

How many times had Sherlock decided he would drop a case only to pick it up again when inspiration stuck? Surely John should have expected this.

To be fair, Sherlock had already changed his mind about the case twice.

John had accepted the first change when Sherlock had dragged him into that strangely untouched flat despite initially refusing the case. He'd been willing to go along with the whole thing, even when he'd found himself getting too emotionally invested, but this time Sherlock hadn't just changed his mind again, he'd lied about it, too.

There were passages on the table that John didn't recognise, passages that Sherlock had never discussed with him. Sherlock also hadn't told him that he was getting new portraits made, or that he had been researching another city. Why? On the very unlikely assumption that Gloria could possibly still be alive? That made no sense.

This trip had been pitched to John as something entirely different – a belated honeymoon, a chance for them to be together for a while without the intrusion of work. Not that John minded the work. He was just worn out, and he wanted more quality time with the man he loved. John's heart ached that Sherlock thought that meant he couldn't be honest with him.

But then, it wasn't as if he was being honest with Sherlock.

Had he ever been entirely honest with anyone at all?

Only an hour ago they'd been reminiscing about childhood holidays and John had failed to tell Sherlock the truth even about that. Of all the people in his life, Sherlock was certainly the one most likely to believe him, or at least not call him insane, but John just couldn't bring himself to tell the truth.

John had been talking about one of the most interesting events of his entire life and he'd sanitised it down to nothing but boredom. True, the last half of the holiday had been all bird watching and tennis on the telly…

Those first three days, though.

John had had a wonderful adventure during those days, real 'Swallows and Amazons' stuff with his new best friend – climbing cliffs, exploring caves, swimming in hidden pools, and all around having the time of his life.

Until his mother put a stop to all that.

At the time John hadn't understood.

He'd thought then that she might have objected to him making a friend amongst the unknown locals, or maybe she'd just decided that Matthew was a bad influence himself. She'd told him not to go exploring the cliffs, and for all she knew it was Matthew who'd instigated it all.

The sheer scale of her upset had seemed so unfair to John at the time.

Matthew had clearly known those tunnels like the back of his hand, and John had always come out again in time for dinner. It wasn't until the argument he had with his brother six months later that he had actually begun to understand what had really happened.

And how deathly serious the whole incident had been.

Summer, 1994 – Yorkshire Coast

The sun was hot, far hotter than John expected on the east coast at this time of year.

There'd been a time, before the divorce and his father disappearing, when the family would have spent these two weeks in Florida. Days filled with theme parks, golden beaches and fast food he'd only ever seen in the movies. Real fun.

All his memories of those holidays were fading now, becoming vague impressions of heat, glittering lights, and a man who was rapidly becoming little more than a shadow in his mind.

These days they holidayed at home. Exhilarating flights to far off countries became long boring train journeys to the tired coastal resort where their mother would rent a cottage from friends. It was all they could afford.

At least the weather was warm this year. Too warm, really.

The tide was going out and his brother was following it, hunting amongst the rock pools for something interesting to tease. That didn't seem like much fun.

Unlike Henry, who had inherited their father's ability to tan easily,

John had their mum's 'pale and interesting' look. With his dark hair it seemed only natural that he'd turn a nice nut brown in the sun, but instead he could feel the skin on his back tightening after only half an hour.

John lifted a hand damp with seawater to his neck to cool it but the salt burned his skin. He hadn't put any sunscreen on and now he was going to pay.

He watched Henry for a moment, then turned to look at the cliffs.

The sun was still rising, leaving almost no shade on that muddy brown rock face. To his left, where the poor excuse for a beach turned into a true rocky scree, the cliffs shifted from brown to the dull grey-white of chalk. At the base dark shadows suggested possible routes into tunnels, interesting adventures out of the sun.

Though there were red warning signs standing like guards amongst the rocks, a quick glance at the beach showed him that there were no adults in sight to make him read them.

He waved briefly to Henry, confident that his brother wouldn't give him away so long as John didn't reveal Henry's own plan to catch an octopus to keep in the bathtub at home.

The rocks were sharp and slippery, a recent fall from the cliffs that had yet to be worn smooth by the tide. There was no obvious path through that John could see, but he was strong and fast on his feet. He felt sure he could cross them easily.

His confidence served him well until he'd almost reached the nearest shadow. It was a cave, just as he'd hoped, with an entrance large enough for a small boy of ten to walk into without stooping. Unfortunately the large flat rock sitting just inside was perfectly balanced to send a boy like that tumbling backwards towards the jagged stones below.

A voice shouted, 'On your left!'

Moving without any conscious instructions from his brain, John's left hand reached out and grabbed the tuft of samphire growing from the cliff face. It wasn't much of a handhold, but it was enough to change his balance.

John threw himself forward into the cave, laughing from the shock as he landed with a squelch on the slimy stones. He wasn't hurt! What an adventure!

The cave smelled terrible, a horrid rotten odour that John put down to the thick slippery layer of seaweed underfoot. He sat up, determined to get his face away from the smell, then gasped at the sight above him.

He'd seen stories about cave painting before but he never thought he would see it for real. But there, four feet up the wall of the cave entrance, was a series of small dark brown handprints.

Beside the marks a boy stood watching him.

'You nearly had a nasty fall,' he said, with a chilling kind of conviction that almost distracted John from his wonder. 'You should be more careful.'

'I will be. Thanks for the help.'

The boy nodded and looked towards the mouth of the cave. 'It took me a while to notice the plants when I came here. I didn't want you to go the same way.'

John nodded vaguely. He didn't really know what to say to that, so he tried to use the good manners his mother was always reminding him about.

'I'm John,' he said, holding out his hand.

Instead of shaking it the boy just looked at him.

Outside the distant sound of waves and gulls made the silence all the more uncomfortable.

'Matthew,' he replied, at last, as if he hadn't remembered the word until then.

John swallowed and wondered what else to say. He didn't usually have trouble making friends, but something about Matthew made him uneasy.

'How long have you been coming here?' he asked. Maybe the boy could show him around.

'I found the entrance last week…' Matthew said. Suddenly he smiled. 'There's a hidden pool back there, wanna see?'

The tunnels were dark but they began to climb after the first few metres, just enough to be dry and sandy instead of disgustingly wet.

Matthew chatted away behind him, describing the various fish and crabs he'd found in the pool.

It wasn't until they'd been walking for at least ten minutes that John realised he could no longer see anything at all. His new companion had seemed so confident that John hadn't noticed the deepening shadows, but now he wasn't sure he'd spot the pool before he was stepping into it.

He was starting to worry more and more about his footing, about the spiders and other things that could be hiding in the dark, about being trapped, when they stepped out into a large open space.

High above, he could see small grass-fringed holes in the ceiling of the cave, probably leading out to the fields above the cliffs. Bright beautiful shafts of light streamed down to glitter on the slightly rippling surface of the water.

John bent down and touched it, shivering a little at the cold after the bright sun outside. The pool was massive, and while the foul smell lingered, it didn't seem to come from the water. It was fresh, not salt water. Maybe it was fed by a spring, or a stream that had eaten through the chalk.

He didn't know much of anything about nature, but he knew it felt like a wonderful temptation. The sunburn on his back stung as he straightened up, the pain making his decision for him.

Grinning back at Matthew he half jumped, half flopped into the water, gasping at the sudden temperature change. Matthew smiled happily and dove in after him.

The pair played together until John heard the echoes of his brother calling for him from the beach below.

John hadn't wanted to leave. Despite his initial disquiet – still not really gone, to be fair – he'd found Matthew to be just the kind of holiday friend he'd always hoped for, and he only agreed to go when the boy promised to meet him there again the next day.

The two days that followed were glorious.

John had rarely had so much fun in his life, even during those dimly remembered holidays in Florida. Free from the watchful eyes of adults he and Matthew played all the dangerous games they could imagine, leaping from high rocks and diving deep under the water's surface.

A favourite contest between them was to retrieve slimy treasures from the depths. His mother would never let John keep anything he brought home, always complaining about some phantom smell that John was sure she was exaggerating. He knew she'd always been a stickler for cleanliness, so he'd taken to leaving them in a bucket by the back door, but the items were always gone by morning.

He didn't mind, there were plenty of opportunities to find more, and other ways they could play. His mother might worry about how grazed his skin was getting, but John knew he was safe playing with Matthew, no matter how risky their stunts might seem.

The only rule they had was to avoid the far shore, where the light didn't quite reach and the awful smell seemed to be strongest. Matthew seemed reluctant to go over there. John didn't blame him – why leave the pleasant side of the pool and have to breathe that in all day?

As the winds picked up outside the cave, whistling and moaning through the holes above them and sending the occasional splatter of rain down on their heads, John failed to hear his brother shouting. He'd left his watch – a treasured bright green Swatch – by the side of the pool and didn't remember to check it until he heard a rumble of thunder and a voice that sounded eerily like his mother calling for him.

He turned to Matthew to ask if the other boy heard the voice, too, but his companion was gone. The sky had darkened with this sudden summer storm and John could barely see his way around the cave now. The water seemed to be still. He could only hear his own breathing. There was no sign of Matthew other than the scuffed sand around the tunnel entrance.

A flash of lightning lit up the space, just for an instant, and John saw him at last.

Matthew was sitting on the other bank with his back to the wall, watching him.

John was about to call out to him when he heard the voice outside screaming his name again. It was definitely his mother, and she did not sound happy. Perhaps Matthew was scared of the storm, or maybe he just didn't want to face an angry adult.

Either way, the boy knew the caves better than John did, and John didn't dare leave his mother waiting a moment longer. John waved, promised to be back tomorrow, and went on his way.

He never did get to go back to the cave.

His mother was near hysterics by the time John had climbed gingerly down the cliff face between the endlessly criss-crossing rivulets of water.

The tide was coming in, lapping further up the rocks than John had ever previously noticed. He was forced to cut across the higher rocks that he'd been able to avoid before, and every time he slipped his mother let out a terrified gasp from behind her hands. If anything, that noise made the climb more difficult than the water.

With all the self-assurance of a child who has never fallen, John resented that lack of confidence in his skills. In fact, he was so pleased with himself when he reached the ground in front of her that he totally forgot why she was mad.

Sadly for him, his mother's relief at his safe return did not make her forget her panic at his disappearance. She all but dragged him back up the cliff path to where Henry was waiting for them, drenched and miserable.

To punctuate her lecture about the dangers of climbing and wandering off on his own she shook him gently at every pause, as if the movement might drive some sense into him.

'What if you had fallen?' Shake. 'What would you have done then, up there all alone?' Shake. 'You didn't even tell Henry where you were going! No one would ever find you up there!' Shake. 'What if you'd gotten too hurt to climb back down?'

John pulled away, just before she could shake him again. 'It's fine, mum! I've been going up there since Monday! And Matthew found his way around last week, so it must be fine!'

'Who?' His mother had stopped, too, and was looking at him with a face as pale as milk.

'My new friend Matthew! I found the entrance, but he showed me how to get to the pool inside.' As he said it John knew he should feel guilty about giving away the other boy's secrets, but for once he didn't feel bad about sharing the details with his mother.

'What does he look like? This Matthew?'

'Um…about this big,' he began, indicating a height slightly taller than himself, 'dark hair, dark eyes, sort of Spanish looking?…thinner than me…' He faltered, unsure what else to say. 'Red swimming trunks and a scar down the middle of his chest. He likes to fish. And watch *Byker Grove* on the telly.'

She stared at him, her expression caught somewhere between confused and angry, until Henry shouted to them both that he was too cold and wanted to go home.

During the walk back to the cottage the family was silent, Henry sulking and angry that John had made him wait in the rain; John worried that he was going to be grounded; their mother oddly distant.

The storm ended as suddenly as it had begun, and by the time they reached the post office at the edge of the village both brothers' clothes were practically steaming in the warm evening sun.

'Wait there,' their mother told them before ducking into the building without an explanation. John stood by the door and tried to watch her as the postmaster handed her the phone, but she kept her back turned toward him.

Beside him Henry read out the details of all the hand-written adverts in the window, trying to make lewd jokes out of as many of them as possible. John ignored him until Henry said something entirely different.

'Have you seen this boy?' Henry asked in a poor imitation of an actor in a film neither of them was supposed to have seen yet. 'Look! It's a genuine wanted poster! I wonder what he did?'

John looked at it, frowning at the smeared writing where the condensation inside the window had made the ink run. There was a grainy black and white photograph of what might have been a face, and a description that was impossible to read. It might have been anyone at all.

So why did it seem familiar?

Their mother had returned then, ushering them back to the cottage with a pinched expression and not a single word of explanation.

That night, when they should have been in bed, John had sat on the floor by the door of their room to eavesdrop on his mother and the two police officers sitting solemnly in the living room. But he fell asleep again with his face against the doorframe without hearing a single word he could understand.

JOHN 'SAW' THINGS. He hated to put it like that. He hated the whole damn thing, but he especially hated that vaguely sinister phrasing.

It sounded like the opening sentence of a psychiatric assessment, the sort of thing that could end his career – both military and medical. There were treatments, of course, for those who suffered from persistent hallucinations, but the people receiving such treatments were not usually trusted to be out on the battlefield.

Besides, he didn't have hallucinations. He just saw things.

Now that definitely sounded like something from an assessment. If a patient had told him that he would probably have underlined it twice and scheduled some kind of intervention.

Therein lay the problem – he would never believe another person if they told him about experiences identical to his own, so why was he so adamant in believing himself?

Because it didn't happen often?

Because once he'd reached his twenties he'd learned to spot the things that weren't quite real and deal with them without drawing attention to himself?

Because there wasn't another living soul who knew about what he saw?

No. Because he was stubborn. He'd given everything to become a doctor and the occasional strange encounter wasn't going to take that from him.

And it hadn't.

In fact, one such incident was the only reason he was still alive and dozing here on this train with his head resting on Sherlock's shoulder.

There would be no more combat roles for him. But if he hadn't turned his head to look at the dead girl waving from the side of the road then there would have been no more roles of any kind at all, other than as guest of honour at his own damn funeral.

John saw things. Sometimes they spoke to him, too. He wished they wouldn't.

CHAPTER TWO

Present Day – York

JOHN WOKE AGAIN TO FIND HIS CHEEK STILL GLUED TO SHERLOCK'S shoulder by an undignified patch of drool.

He felt groggy and muddled, like he'd slept for hours without getting any real rest. There was barely more than an hour's journey between Peterborough and York, not nearly enough to justify that sickly kind of feeling.

Maybe he should give up the caffeine, or develop a sensible work/life balance. They hadn't had an active case in weeks but he still worked too many hours to ever feel properly rested.

Well, Sherlock had told him they had no active cases.

The documents pertaining to Gloria's case had vanished from the table but John knew he hadn't dreamt them.

A tinny automated voice repeated its announcement that the train would soon be arriving in York.

Feeling a little chagrined, John glanced up at his partner's profile through his lashes, wondering what Sherlock thought of him for apparently sleeping through the entire journey. But Sherlock was watching the buildings zipping past the window with every sign of enjoyment. He didn't seem any more aware of John's awkward position than he had been at the last station.

Reassured by Sherlock's indifference, John yawned, wincing as first his jaw and then his neck cracked in protest of his poor sleeping habits.

'Good morning, sunshine,' Sherlock said without turning his head.

John could just see the glitter of a grin as Sherlock pulled an old-fashioned handkerchief from an inside pocket. Long fingers mopped at his own shoulder for a moment before the square of cotton was offered to John.

So much for not being noticed.

He took it with poor grace and swiped grumpily at the dampness on his face.

'You could have woken me up, you know,' he said. He'd meant to sound irritable, but the muffling effect of the handkerchief just made him indistinct.

'Why? You looked peaceful, I was comfortable.' Sherlock waved his hands as if he was shooing away John's bad mood like a literal rain cloud. As usual, it worked, and John smiled despite himself.

'I didn't see any reason to disturb you.'

Turning in his seat John did his best to clean up the mess on Sherlock's shoulder. 'I was drooling on you!'

'You often drool on me, John. Any time your shoulder hurts enough that you have to sleep with your head on my chest, you drool on me – right here.' Sherlock gestured to a point just over his heart.

Before John could comment on the sweetness of the image, Sherlock spoiled it by continuing, 'And whenever you pretend to watch the Grand Prix to punish me for keeping you up for days on a case, you fall asleep with your head on my knee but you always end up drooling right on my–'

'Yes, thank you,' John said loudly to cover the word 'crotch'.

Judging by the scandalised expression of the woman sitting opposite, he hadn't been quite loud enough.

Sherlock chuckled slightly when she grabbed her bag and headed towards the train doors ahead of the crowds.

'Have you been messing with her the entire time I was asleep?'

'No.' The grin surfaced again before Sherlock could suppress it.

John groaned. 'Sherlock–'

'I was just holding your hand, I swear.'

'Oh, well, I suppose that was–'

'Of course,' Sherlock went on, reaching over to take John's hand where it rested in his lap, 'from where she was sitting it probably looked like something else entirely.'

With his free hand John pinched the bridge of his nose in frustration. 'Oh my god.'

Beside him Sherlock laughed and leaned in to press a kiss under his ear. John turned to capture those lips for himself. It had been at least an hour since he'd last been kissed, and whether this was a real honeymoon or not, John intended to make the most of it.

SITTING IN A QUIET Georgian terrace just outside of the ancient city walls, the guest house looked much like any other in the row. Inside the house was a baffling rabbit's warren of interconnected rooms. John wouldn't have been all that surprised to open a window and find himself looking out onto another town entirely.

He was just wondering whether the house featured in one of the city's famous ghost tours when the landlady proudly showed them the bomb damage that had been left on one window ledge after World War Two.

'They say there's an old family legend,' she said, 'that the girls who were sleeping in here were frightened out of bed by a ghost just before a lump of masonry flew in through the window. But everyone else says they woke up because of the air raid sirens. You know how children are.'

When she went on to point out the park at the end of the street where three homes had been destroyed, John found himself wishing that they'd booked into a building with less history, regardless of how charming the guest house might be. He knew what old homes like this could have inside.

Of course, London had seen more than its fair share of blitz damage, but London was a living city. The march of progress had wiped away many of the more domestic reminders of the war. Sherlock could identify the changes in architecture, the disjointed meetings of old and new that were the city's scars, but John had never been as aware of the history as he was right here.

They'd passed a church on their journey from the station that had been preserved in its post-blitz state. A hollow, empty memorial. Something at the guest house had the same kind of vibe.

With a shudder John turned away to see Sherlock surreptitiously measuring the depth of a wall with his thumb. At least Sherlock seemed to be loving the place.

On the way up the stairs John had noticed Sherlock quietly noting the measurements and looking, as always, for hidden spaces. Sherlock had a fascination for all the secret and forgotten places that peppered homes of this age. It was an interest that John could tolerate right up until Sherlock tried to climb into any of them.

He didn't want to explain to an entirely different fire brigade why his beloved husband had believed he could fit up the chimney. At least the service in London were used to them.

Besides, the soot always made him sneeze and Sherlock's hair had a preternatural capacity for attracting any kind of dust. It made kissing him after any such adventure less than pleasant.

John's brain faded out for a minute as it reminded him of the merits of getting Sherlock in the shower. Though he was sure that could be arranged without an architectural misadventure.

There was a cough behind him and John realised he'd been caught staring at his partner like a lovesick but exasperated puppy. He gave the landlady a half-apologetic smile before he let his gaze drift to the open door of their room.

Suddenly grand tours of strange old houses had lost their appeal. There was a king-size four-poster bed in there, and he swore it had his name written all over it. Both their names, in fact.

'Thank you for the tour,' he said, trying to mask the eagerness in his voice with genuine warmth, 'but it was a long train journey, so we'd like to rest for a while before we go out in search of dinner.'

For once Sherlock understood the message in John's subtly raised eyebrows.

He nodded enthusiastically. 'Oh yes, we're very tired.'

The landlady seemed disappointed at having her well-rehearsed spiel interrupted, but she headed for the stairs all the same.

'Well, you boys just ask if you want to know more about the history of this place. No one else here knows it quite as well as me.'

John was just about to close the door behind them when she called up to them from the next landing.

'Don't forget there's no food allowed in the rooms! I don't want to have to clean takeaway grease stains off all my sheets!'

John shut the door before Sherlock could say anything about not planning on staining the sheets with food.

Sherlock gave him a lewd grin anyway. Maybe this trip was going to be more honeymoon-like than he had thought.

THE BED WAS just as soft and comfortable as it had looked, and, to his embarrassment, John was out like a light almost the instant his head touched the pillow.

He woke what seemed like a short time later, feeling terrible that he had fallen asleep when Sherlock was clearly in a flirtatious mood. Once the door had been shut, Sherlock had wasted no time in stripping John of his coat and shoes while kissing every bit of neck he could reach. John had only meant to close his eyes while Sherlock ducked into the bathroom, but instead he'd gone to sleep.

That couldn't have looked good. Sherlock was a confident guy, but your spouse falling asleep hours into your sort-of-honeymoon before you'd managed much more than a few gentle kisses? It wasn't exactly sexy.

John sighed and stretched, staring at the ceiling. Had Sherlock waited for him to wake up, or was he out looking for clues on this case he said he wasn't even working on?

Gloria's case, as they'd come to call it, had been a strange one. John had woken in the middle of a rare day off nearly a month ago to find two people already meeting with Sherlock in the living room.

They'd claimed to be worried about the whereabouts of their missing aunt, Gloria Evans. Or, rather, they were concerned with claiming an inheritance that had ended up on the Bona Vacantia lists. An heir hunter had found them and told them that either they or Gloria were due to inherit a good sum of money from the death of some far distant relative. But evidence of the aunt could not be traced.

Given her age she could well be dead, but there was no death certificate for her anywhere.

In fact, the clients, Ian and Jessica, had claimed to have never heard of Gloria until they were contacted by the heir hunter.

All they'd had was a pile of old documents for her. A haphazardly copied family tree. The details of a man who'd died intestate a decade earlier. An unsigned contract with an heir hunting firm that included a clause prohibiting precisely the contact they were proposing with Sherlock. A faded photograph, the colours distorted by age and sunlight but still clearly showing a young black woman with a very seventies Afro. And, finally, a small envelope containing nothing but tiny scrapes of what turned out to be a torn-up greeting card.

It had been implied that they'd never heard of this woman because of their mother's racism – they were both blonde and had looked nothing like the woman in the photograph.

Sherlock had initially turned down the case because he suspected the clients were being less than honest, but additional information had piqued his interest and led to further investigation once before.

It seemed that now something new – that John hadn't seen yet – had led Sherlock to York.

'Ah, sleeping beauty, awake at last. Hello, darling.'

John was relieved to see that Sherlock was standing in the bathroom doorway, silhouetted by dull grey light.

Was it early morning already? Or just dusk? John couldn't remember which side of the house their room was on.

He tipped his head in Sherlock's direction and tried to make out the shape of him in the dimness. Tall and thin as always, but maybe a little thinner than usual. John blinked, concerned for Sherlock's health for a moment before he realized that his husband was merely naked.

That was a nice surprise.

'Hey.' His hand was heavy as he raised it, sleep clinging to him like cobwebs, making him sluggish. He was far too comfortable to leave the bed just yet, but he knew that he would feel even better if he weren't alone. 'C'mere.'

Sherlock smiled, teeth glinting slightly, and glanced back at something. A bright light filled the bathroom as Sherlock checked his phone, and confirmed the nudity that John had suspected a moment before. Well, he was mostly nude. For some reason that John couldn't entirely fathom, Sherlock was still wearing the loosely tied cravat around his neck. The soft purple of the silk did look good against his skin.

He was too busy admiring the sight in front of him to hear what Sherlock said.

'I said, do you want to get something to eat before bed?' Sherlock repeated, with a knowing smirk.

'Do I look like I want something to eat?' John asked, waving a hand at his own reclining form. 'Other than you?'

Sherlock shook a teasing finger at him. 'Aren't you the one who's always telling me about the value of regular meals?'

'Since when have you been the one that listens?' John laughed, his tone as low and gentle.

The light of the phone screen blinked out, throwing them into a darkness that seemed deeper than it had before. Though he could see less, John still felt a little more comfortable knowing that Sherlock was waiting there in the dark.

John heard more than felt the rasp of Sherlock's callused fingertips trailing along the top of his foot and up his calf. The grooves worn by years of violin practice caught at the fabric of his jeans in a way that felt so unique to the two of them. John had never had this with anyone else, this clear and constant awareness of how his beloved affected every sense.

He shivered as Sherlock's fingertips reached his knee.

Two years of disparate sleep patterns had taught John to follow Sherlock's progress around the flat by sound alone, but there was always a special thrill when sound finally became touch.

Beneath him the bed dipped where Sherlock leaned over him.

Hot lips found a thin sliver of skin between belt and shirt, kissing softly, while a slightly chilly nose nuzzled against the trail of hair beneath his belly button.

'I listen,' Sherlock said, his breath causing goosebumps across John's belly, 'when the information is needed.'

John felt his arm hairs raise an instant before Sherlock nipped at him.

Suddenly his jeans were far too tight for the situation.

Sherlock bit him again, a little harder, sucking hard to leave a circle of warmth that would be a bruise by morning.

'Ah!' John gasped, his hands coming up to stroke over Sherlock's hair, apparently of their own volition. 'A-and this is what counts as needed – my secondary erogenous zones?'

'Very.' The word was punctuated on the 'r' with a pointed swipe of Sherlock's tongue over John's navel.

It seemed that while he'd slept, Sherlock had taken a shower. His hair was hanging in long soft strands that curled around John's fingers. Even after all this time, it still was strange to feel his hair moving like that, free from the gel that Sherlock used to avoid washing it during cases and the occasional periods of depression that kept him in bed for days.

John tugged gently at Sherlock's hair, letting his nails scratch soothingly over the scalp behind his ears. He wanted to kiss Sherlock properly now, and take full advantage of that rare curtain of untamed hair. There was something romantic about feeling it brushing across his cheeks as it formed a screen from the rest of the world. Nothing but the two of them in that soft, dark space filled with the rhythms of their own breathing.

He groaned deep as Sherlock gave his stomach one last parting nip before he edged forward.

John pulled a little harder at his hair, trying to urge him to move at a faster pace.

The gesture had no effect. As always, Sherlock would do as he liked.

The tip of Sherlock's nose warmed as he traced a path up John's torso with it, following the trail of fuzz over his belly and pushing the hem of his shirt up along the way. One fine-boned hand slipped under the fabric to stroke firmly over John's ribs, while the hand that had stilled on his thigh turned to trace the inner seam of John's jeans.

Giving up on Sherlock's hair for now, John let his hands stroke softly over the sharp angles of his face, neck, and collarbones, not gripping any more, just mapping the shape of him in this moment. All he could see in the deepening darkness was the fall of his hair and the narrow lines of his shoulders. He wished he could reach the lights, but the mood was too relaxed for him to risk disturbing it.

The bed springs creaked and the mattress sank another inch as Sherlock swung his legs up to straddle John's hips.

John wanted to kick his jeans down his legs and away. He wanted to strip completely and roll Sherlock onto his back. He wanted to do a million impulsive things, but sleepiness kept him still under Sherlock's weight.

Sherlock leaned down over him then, finally creating that soft curtain of privacy John had been craving. The kiss was long and messy, all lazy sweeping tongues and soft wordless sounds while John traced the lines of Sherlock's back.

He wasn't chasing anything in particular, not yet. That wasn't important to either of them just now.

What mattered was the building warmth wherever their skin met, the paths of their fingers, every meeting of lips and breath and heartbeat.

John tightened his grip over Sherlock's ribs, determined to leave four crescent marks from his nails just as Sherlock had marked his belly with his teeth.

In response, Sherlock hummed and dropped his head to nuzzle against the soft skin below John's ear. John hadn't cut his own hair since his medical discharge from the army, amused by the way the less formal style had changed the shape of his face. Now it curled thickly in a messy mop that tickled Sherlock's nose, making him huff against his neck in a futile effort to escape from it.

The irritated noise made John chuckle.

Sherlock tried to growl, only to huff again as more hair brushed over his face.

Perhaps it was the exhaustion, or the lingering pull of sleep, but, whatever the reason, John found the hilarity of the situation building in his chest. Soft chuckles turned into giggling, which irritated Sherlock more.

John groaned as Sherlock nipped at his neck as if he were trying to remind him of exactly what they were doing. Always the contrary one, John gave up his grip on Sherlock's ribs only to let his fingertips dance across his skin.

'Ah! You! Fuck!' This time it was Sherlock who swore in a heated gasp. While John was still mostly dressed, Sherlock was entirely naked but for that cravat. It seemed from Sherlock's hitching breaths that wriggling away from John's hand had been more stimulating than expected.

In response, John redoubled his efforts, tickling with both hands between joyful gasping laughs.

There was a moment of chaos where Sherlock writhed, apparently caught between escaping and enjoying the sensations, before he managed to grab John's wrists.

'Sherl…oh…' John cut himself off with a sigh, his fingers twitching uselessly where they were held an inch away from Sherlock's skin. Through his jeans he could feel the perfect heat and weight of his almost perfect husband. The fabric separating them suddenly felt like an intolerable gulf.

'Are you going to behave?' Sherlock asked, with every ounce of hauteur his slim frame possessed.

John licked his lips, glancing away into the dark around them. He wasn't sure if Sherlock could see him in the darkness, but he felt that the gesture gave some semblance of truth to his act. Besides, Sherlock could probably feel his posture even through their limited points of contact. He hummed as if considering his options.

'Well?' Sherlock tightened his fingers on John's wrists to highlight the question.

'No.' John shook his head, planted his feet firmly against the mattress and flipped them in a single seamless roll.

Pinned now beneath John's weight, Sherlock flexed his hips, not in an attempt to escape but just to drive his captor mad with insufficient friction.

'Bastard,' Sherlock muttered against John's collarbone. 'Evil, unfair, cheating, devious–'

'Handsome,' John lazily offered as he stroked Sherlock's hair back from his face.

'Conceited...'

A startled bark of laughter echoed through the room in the face of Sherlock's barefaced hypocrisy. There was no point challenging him, it would only encourage him.

For all Sherlock's complaints, his hands had still found their way into the space between them, his thumb pressing lazily at the first button on John's jeans.

Perhaps he should encourage him, after all.

JOHN WOKE TO the pleasant ache of an hour well spent and a slight sense of embarrassment at apparently falling asleep in the afterglow.

It was immediately obvious from the chill of his skin that he hadn't dozed off for just a short period – he must have laid there without any covers for quite a while. He hoped after two years Sherlock knew him well enough not to be too offended.

At first he thought it was the cold that woke him, and stifling a yawn he pulled his sweat-damp shirt off over his head with his eyes shut.

His brain didn't consciously register the change in light as the shirt passed in front of his face, but when he turned to climb under the sheets, some neglected ancient animal sense told him that something about the room had changed.

He reluctantly opened his eyes, the lure of sleep and his husband's warmth far more tempting than all but the strongest survival instincts.

Sherlock was asleep beside him, the deep regular snores he swore he didn't make rumbling against the pillow. Beyond his shadowy figure the curtains were still drawn. The lights were off and the bathroom door had been closed to cut off the light from that window.

The room should have been dark. There certainly shouldn't have been a small orange light flickering a foot above the sheets, down beyond John's feet.

There was, though, because a dead woman was sitting at the end of their bed holding a candle.

The woman looked up at the small noises from the bed as John turned his head towards her.

She seemed to be young, and though the candle added a warm glow to her skin, she was pale in a way that living people never were.

She had to be dead. Young women in floor-length corseted gowns and mob-caps didn't usually appear in his bedroom uninvited. In fact, in his life so far this particular scenario had never happened, though he'd seen other visions like this in the strangest places over the years.

Sherlock had once said that the improbable was preferable to the impossible, but since he'd played in caves with a dead boy long ago, John had a slightly different definition of impossible.

He also had a lot less patience for the impossible than Sherlock did.

John was tired. He was cold. He'd just had fantastic sex with his fantastic husband and he had absolutely no interest in indulging whatever this newcomer's tragic backstory might be. With ghosts there was always a tragic backstory.

He'd long since realised that there wasn't time enough in the world to engage with every bygone tragedy, and certainly not enough sanity. The real world was the living world, the one he resided in, and the dead were merely visiting. Maybe it was selfish, but John only had so much energy to go around.

There was a difference between helping the freshly dead and someone like this. Her clothes looked Georgian – there couldn't possibly be anyone alive who remembered her, or whose life could be affected by whatever story she had to tell.

Decision made, he waved a sleepy hand at the woman and turned over to burrow underneath the sheets where he could get as close to Sherlock as possible.

Sherlock was warm and real.

Right now, in the middle of the night, that was all that mattered.

As if in proof of Sherlock's own vitality, the snoring continued unabated even when John slipped a cold arm around his waist.

He would pretend that the thing at the end of the bed was just a dream, just like he had with most of his visions over the last twenty years or so.

Closing his eyes tight against the unwelcome light, John forced his breathing to follow the rhythm of Sherlock's snores and soon drifted back into an uneasy sleep.

At the bottom of the bed the candle flame flickered until morning, when the nearby peals of the Minster's dawn bells finally convinced her to leave. John dimly registered her departure, his brain only briefly surfacing from sleep before the bells lulled him under again.

CHAPTER THREE

Spring, 1995 – Smethwick, East Midlands

FROM SOMEWHERE OFF TO JOHN'S LEFT CAME THE SOFT, FAST RINGING of a tiny bell, every tinkling noise coinciding with the pat of a paw against concrete.

'Here, kitty, kitty!' he murmured under his breath, holding his hand out a few inches above the wall of number 27 just as they passed by on their way home from school.

Precisely on cue Marble jumped up onto the wall, her soft fuzzy head slotting perfectly into the curve of his palm. She was an old cat, her joints turned stiff with age and one leg dragging behind her a little as she ran, but she could always keep up with him.

This was their daily ritual – whatever time he finished school she'd always be waiting for him. From number 27 to the conifer hedge at number 51 they'd walk together, cat and boy, him scratching her ears and her meowing her contentment until it was time to separate again.

Henry didn't like it.

Henry hadn't liked a lot of things since their boring summer holiday. Yes, it had sucked that their mum had banned them both from going out without her, but it was February now! How could he still be angry with John after all this time?

Still, John had learned to lower his voice when he spoke to Marble, and to try not to do anything else that might irritate Henry even more. It was hard to know what might annoy him when it seemed like everything could set him off at any moment.

Marble made a soft meeping noise as she leapt across the gap left by an open gate.

John muttered a little praise and ran his hand down her bony spine.

'Stop it.'

John looked at Henry in confusion, never breaking his stride.

'You're nearly eleven, John, don't you think you're too old for all that crap?' Henry spat.

Although he was talking to John, he wasn't looking at him, his eyes turning to watch a leaf blowing across the road like it was the most fascinating thing he'd ever seen.

'What? Stroking a cat?' John asked incredulously. 'Since when is anyone 'too old' to be nice to—'

'She's been dead for five years! Stop playing these sick games of make believe!' Henry finally looked at him. His eyes were filled with unshed tears. 'You're too old for imaginary friends and you're scaring the shit out of mum!'

Suddenly Henry shoved John in the chest, pushing him back until he collided with the wall. At his elbow Marble hissed in irritation before she jumped into the rose bush on the other side of the wall and disappeared.

'I don't know why you thought it was funny to tell mum that you saw the kid who died in those caves, but I'm telling you now to stop it.' Henry's voice was cold and empty, and so, so angry.

John stared at him, so confused that he felt like the ground was going to melt away from under his feet and prove that the world wasn't real any more.

'That's impossible.'

Marble had just been under his fingertips, just like she had been every day for years. Yes, he did vaguely remember when she was knocked down by the postie's van just before his sixth birthday but...she'd been fine afterwards, more or less. Her leg had never been right again, but that's what had made him want to be a vet in the first place.

The dream of becoming a vet had vanished after he was charged by an entire herd of sheep at age eight, so he'd decided to be a doctor since that was still the same sort of thing. He'd just be working with animals that listened to reason. Some of the time, anyway.

'Look.' Henry bit his lip and breathed hard through his nose, as if he was trying to calm himself. 'If you won't do it for me, or mum, please, do it for yourself. You're going up to comp next year, and I can't protect you there.'

'I don't need protecting,' John said, with a tone of bravado that he really didn't feel. He'd been dreading comprehensive school for months, and there wasn't long left now. Still, he didn't want or need his brother's protection, whatever was going on.

John pushed past him and headed for home, keeping his eyes open for Marble's shape amongst the garden shrubbery.

She wasn't there. Not that day, or ever again.

Present Day – York

JOHN WOKE AGAIN to a painfully empty stomach in an equally empty bed. The sense of unreality around time that he had noticed last night was still lingering, so that somehow, he simultaneously felt like he'd slept for days and not at all.

At least the sounds of the shower running in the next room was proof that Sherlock wasn't far away. There was always a risk with Sherlock that he might have vanished. It was good to know his husband would be with him again soon.

What a shame that the landlady's ban on outside food meant that breakfast would be a little further from his reach.

Would breakfast be provided here? John hadn't been involved in booking the guest house so he didn't know, and Sherlock was so cavalier about food that he probably didn't know either.

He stared at the ceiling, listening to his stomach growling and silently debating the benefits of getting out of bed.

There wasn't much point yet, not while the shower was still occupied, anyway. He was warm under the sheets, and the shower cubicle wasn't nearly big enough to fit them both. Even if it had been, John was far too hungry to risk Sherlock getting frisky – he'd probably get low blood sugar and pass out. Not that such an undignified thing had ever happened to him before, but given how weirdly tired he was this morning John wasn't going to take the risk.

He was on holiday, whatever Sherlock thought they were doing, and he was going to spend as much of it in a horizontal position as possible.

Outside the window bells started to sound again. That was something he rarely heard in London, certainly not from the comfort of his bed. He'd heard them last night, or he thought he had.

The music was beautiful but not perfect – some kind of practice session perhaps? Every so often a note would be missed or the timing would drift just a little. The dissonance was just enough that instead of focusing on the music, John's brain slipped to the uncomfortable dreams he'd had the night before.

He couldn't exactly call them nightmares. He didn't really have nightmares in the classical sense – his brain didn't seem to be capable of inventing horrors, it just replayed a few of the greatest hits from the back catalogue already in his head.

The disturbing incident involving his brother and Marble had hardly featured in his dreams after he found out about Matthew, and both ghosts had vanished from his dreams around the time he handled his first cadaver. Then he'd joined the army, and all his dreams had taken on a gritty quality, like even his brain was coated in sand he couldn't get away from.

It was odd – given the conversation he'd had with Sherlock about childhood holidays the day before – that his brain had chosen to present him with memories of Marble, and not the boy from the cave. He vaguely thought that he might have dreamt of Matthew on the train, but his dreams were so predictably upsetting that he no longer seemed to remember having them any more.

At least, not when Sherlock was close at hand.

There was something so reassuringly logical about Sherlock, despite his eccentric behaviour, that John's subconscious assumed he was always safe from harm in his presence. Which only proved that John's subconscious was as foolish as the rest of him, since he'd been in just as many dangerous situations with Sherlock as he had been in the army.

Not for the first time he wondered what Sherlock would say if John told him about the strange things in his life.

The things that were stranger than Sherlock himself, anyway.

He chuckled quietly to himself – Sherlock would probably be jealous.

How would that conversation go exactly?

'I petted the neighbours' cat for four years after it died'? Well, that just sounded like amateur taxidermy at best and delusion at worst.

'I unwittingly played with a ghost for three days only a few feet from his corpse' was much, much worse. That sounded like the sort of fantasy a child's mind would create to deal with the trauma – John still believing that story as an adult would be unsettling to any sane person. Hell, it was unsettling to John.

'I've helped you solve more than one case by accidentally talking to the deceased'? Saying that would probably get him divorced. Sherlock took his work very seriously. There was no way John could picture him tolerating that kind of statement. No matter how true it might be.

'A woman spent the night at the end of our bed'. Well that would definitely result in an argument. Sherlock would want to know why she was there, and 'I didn't ask' wouldn't be an acceptable answer.

Someone as curious as Sherlock wouldn't understand John's desire to avoid encouraging that kind of thing. In fact, if Sherlock believed in the afterlife, he would probably actively pursue the dead for clues. John wasn't sure which would be worse.

Ghosts made John uncomfortable. Thinking that phrase made him uncomfortable, too. It made him sound insane, as did his reasoning – he didn't like the emotional shift that came with realising he was speaking to a dead person. There was the residual guilt from what he'd put his mother through, but that was often overwhelmed by the sense of hopelessness that he couldn't possibly help these people. He was a doctor. Helping was what he did.

Even in those instances where communicating with them had changed something, it didn't help them. Matthew's body wasn't in a cave anymore, but he was still dead. Marble was still dead. The trainspotter, the girl in Afghanistan, the dancer, the dogwalker – they were all still dead.

The woman in the mob-cap had sat at the end of the bed all night. She could sit there forever, and it would never make an ounce of difference.

In the next room the shower shut off.

'John?' Sherlock called to him through the closed door, derailing his train of thought. 'The shower's free, I'd get in here before all the hot water gets used up!'

He shook his head as if the gesture could get rid of all the unwanted angst, and rolled out of bed with as much dignity as he could manage.

They'd been together for two years now. The window for any kind of 'hey, I'm insane but sometimes my visions are useful' conversation was well and truly closed.

He needed to get his head back in the game. Get some rest on this so called 'holiday,' get a proper job when they got back to London, and lead as normal a life as any person married to Sherlock Holmes could manage.

CHAPTER FOUR

Three Weeks Ago – Marylebone, London

'I THOUGHT YOU SAID WE WEREN'T TAKING GLORIA'S CASE?'

Sherlock was sitting cross-legged at the windowsill carefully reassembling the remains of the greeting card with tweezers and a roll of tape. John could just see the pink tip of his tongue poking out of his mouth in concentration. He looked adorable, which wasn't a look that came easily to a man with such sharp features and spidery limbs. Or perhaps John was just biased. The fact that Sherlock was all elbows and knees was somehow endearing.

'Oh, we're probably not,' Sherlock said. 'But you were right – we don't have anything else going on right now. Besides, you'll be off to work in a minute.'

It wasn't all that common for Sherlock to have nothing to occupy him – cases seemed to come in packs, almost like buses, but Sherlock was good at multitasking and staggering them out so he was always on the move.

Of course, after a case there was the dreaded paperwork, or worse – court appearances. It was rare for Sherlock to have completely cleared his workload. He probably didn't know what to do with himself.

As if reading his mind, Sherlock sighed dramatically and tipped back to rest against John's legs like a neglected puppy. 'I'll be bored and lonely whilst you're gone.'

John couldn't help but smile at that, not least because he could tell Sherlock was still supporting most of his own weight. Sherlock could always tell when John was having a bad pain day. One of the benefits of being loved by the country's greatest detective,

John thought. There were others, though he couldn't always remember them.

'So, the world's most difficult jigsaw puzzle is an adequate replacement for me?' he teased.

'Oh, no,' Sherlock said, then grinned. 'This isn't nearly the world's most difficult puzzle. Mycroft had a dozen of those growing up. We used to have races to see who could finished them the fastest. This isn't all that difficult. Just small.'

'The madcap adventures of your childhood never cease to amaze me,' John laughed.

He sipped his tea while he watched Sherlock carefully place two more pieces. Whatever he might have said about it not being difficult, John could tell it was still going to take hours.

The television was playing to itself in the background, some story about a police hunt over an attempted murder case. John stared blankly at the screen for a minute or two, but the information wasn't sinking in. It didn't seem like their kind of case, anyway.

He shook his head and wished his tea would wake him up a little faster.

'Well, I can't stand here all day being your backrest, I have to get to the clinic.' He sighed. 'Found anything interesting before I go?'

Sherlock shook his head. 'Only a horrible tableau of Easter-themed pastel animals…and the obvious.'

He waved a hand at the blank side of the card that was currently facing upward. John stared, but it just looked like cardboard, turned brown with age and crisscrossed with bright white lines where the torn edges showed though. He couldn't see any pen or pencil marks, or any indents from writing on another page. It was just blank.

'Fine. Don't tell me,' he said, as Sherlock presented his cheek for a kiss.

'You'll get there,' Sherlock called after him when he headed for the stairs.

'No, I won't, because I'll be thinking about work!'

WORK WAS DULL, in the way that only unending crises can be. A rush of adrenaline might be exciting on its own, but once it turns into a constant state, it no longer energises like it should. Low-key panic becomes a way of life if you let it.

The walk-in clinic was supposed to be for people who needed to be seen urgently and couldn't get a regular doctor's appointment, but weren't in immediate danger. Stomach upsets, ear infections, fevers – that was what he should have been dealing with.

His first case of the day turned out to be a woman in her fifties who was having a heart attack but didn't want to bother 'the nice nurses at A&E.' She weakly argued with John the whole way into the ambulance and called him rude for making such a fuss.

The next was a man with a silicone egg trapped in an orifice such an object shouldn't really have been put into in the first place, certainly not without reading the instructions.

John didn't have the equipment to help the man but at least he could refer him right away. Unfortunately, while he was explaining the procedure the A&E staff would likely have to follow to remove the egg, the patient fainted and caught his head on the edge of John's desk.

A second ambulance in as many patients. He was going to set a new record. Not good for his third week in the job.

The waiting room was looking distinctly nervous.

All of which had made the next patient seem like something of a relief. Calm, relaxed, and making jokes. The man said he had slipped while carving meat the day before. He'd assumed the cut in his arm would heal on its own, but perhaps it needed stitches.

An easy enough job to assess.

The relief was short-lived.

John looked at the proffered arm and forced his face not to move. Sherlock always teased him that he broadcast his emotions but that was just for him – Sherlock was a safe place to show his amazement or confusion or frustration. A battlefield wasn't. A medical office wasn't.

This wound wasn't a day old. It was four or five, at least. It'd been bandaged up well, so it was healing, but the man was right that it had probably needed stitches when it was inflicted.

John kept his head down while he twisted the arm this way and that, pretending to get a better look at the wound. There were fading scratches all over his forearm, while the other wrist bore a large plaster.

He'd been zoning in and out that morning, but the story on the news had mentioned that the attempted murder suspect was likely to require medical attention eventually. He'd had a distinctive wrist tattoo and a host of defensive wounds, most of which would be faded by now. All except for where the girl had stabbed him with his own knife.

It was just John's luck he'd turn up during his shift. Well, he'd dealt with plenty of people who wanted to kill him, or were at least prepared to kill him, so it wasn't a new situation. Just marginally unexpected.

'We can definitely get that sorted out for you!' he said, brightly. 'I just need to get a new sterile suture kit from the store room. Two minutes.'

The man smiled and let him go. Fortunately, it seemed that John wasn't recognisable as a threat and had successfully kept his thoughts off his face. The nameplate on the door that just said 'Locum' helped- certainly some people might recognise his name these days.

It was easy enough to lock the door to the consulting room with his swipe card without drawing the patient's attention.

From there it should have been a simple job for the local police to swoop in and arrest him, but when was John's life ever simple or easy?

For some reason the police stormed in via the waiting room, scattering screaming patients in their wake. The noise alerted the suspect who, on finding the door locked and the windows barred, promptly disappeared into the suspended ceiling.

The rest of John's afternoon was spent in the car park,

answering the same five questions asked a dozen different ways while the suspect rained broken ceiling tiles and cobwebs down on his pursuers.

They finally extracted him, still kicking and screaming, from his hiding place amongst the pipework just after seven, which was long after John's shift should have ended.

He still stayed behind to help the practice manager assess the damage. He'd hoped the clean-up job would be minimal, but they soon found that the threat of asbestos amongst the ruins would force the walk-in clinic to close for at least a week, if not longer.

He trudged home through the rain, texting his contact at the staffing agency and praying there was a role available somewhere that wasn't an emergency department. He'd tried working there before, but his PTSD always reared its head far too quickly.

He should just give in and find a nice steady GP role. He should stop arranging his schedule around Sherlock's cases and get them a regular income. He should grow up.

Instead he bought the largest, unhealthiest pizza the local takeaway could provide and took it home to his husband.

He'd been a grown up once. That had got him shot and nearly taken his leg off.

He'd stick to being immature for a little while longer.

'I CAN'T EAT, I'm on a case,' Sherlock shouted.

John hadn't even reached the top of the stairs yet. He rolled his eyes and fished for his keys – there was no way Sherlock was going to open it for him.

'That's a shame,' he called through the door, 'since this is the kind with the sausage and cheese stuffed crust.'

There was a whine from the sofa as he finally got the door open. Sherlock was laid out on the cushions with his legs running up the wall and his head hanging off the edge.

'Yes, you're definitely far too hard at work to eat anything,' John said, casually dropping the warm pizza box onto Sherlock's chest and sinking gratefully into the space next to him. It was relief to be off his feet at last. He took an ostentatious bite and hummed with pleasure. 'Such a terrible, terrible shame.'

'Fuck the case,' Sherlock said at last, tipping his legs to the side to right himself. 'It's forty years old, anyway.'

'Not exactly what you'd call urgent, then.' John frowned. 'Which case?'

Sherlock's reply was muffled by a mouthful of pepperoni and cheese.

It was true that Sherlock often didn't eat during cases, but his insistence that digestion slowed him down was just a cover for disordered eating. When Sherlock was thinking he forgot everything else. The man was still just as whip-thin as he'd been the day they'd met, but John's habit of buying food Sherlock couldn't entirely resist had certainly given him a much healthier complexion.

Unfortunately the irresistible food was also giving John a little bit of a belly, but he'd deal with that eventually. It was pretty rare for them to get much time between cases, and those usually involved far more running than John would like. John had fully intended to take advantage of the break between cases, but it seemed like Sherlock had already accepted something.

Well, John would indulge tonight. Exercise could wait until tomorrow.

Sherlock balanced the pizza box carefully on the edge of the coffee table, trying to avoid a pile of papers that John recognised as being from Gloria's case.

On the top of the mess sat the now repaired greeting card, all shiny with tape. John's eye settled on it as he chewed.

'I had an exciting day at the clinic…' he began.

'I know,' Sherlock mumbled around the first bite of his second slice, 'saw you on the telly trying not to shout at some poor constable.'

'Oh, god.' If it had been on TV then his family would see it, eventually, and the worried texts would start again. John quietly turned off his phone.

'They didn't say what it was about though, just "apprehending a suspect".'

'What do you think it was?' John asked, a smile creeping onto his face when Sherlock gave an exasperated huff at the obviousness of everything.

'Armed police evacuated a medical facility, so it was someone dangerous.' Sherlock said, punctuating his points with delicate bites of pizza so he could keep speaking clearly. 'You didn't bother to tackle them yourself so it was someone capable of killing, because I know you, John Watson, and you love the drama of a citizen's arrest. And you were pointing at your forearm and wrist while that constable was interviewing you. So it was the suspect in the assault and attempted murder of that student over in Hammersmith.'

John grinned at him and leaned over for a slightly saucy kiss. 'I love it when you do that.'

'I know,' Sherlock preened.

'Anyway, I was going to tell you, because it helped me work out what was up with that card,' John said, pointing to the Easter card.

'Oh? Go on then, explain.'

'Well, the suspect had waited for most of his defensive scratches to heal before he came for help with the knife wound,' John began. 'But he tried to lie about how he got the wound. If he'd really cut himself the day before it would have been either scabbed or still moist, but the wound was pink and mostly healed inside the cut – the skin was still gaping because it was too deep to knit unaided, but the raw edges were healing.'

Sherlock nodded and took another slice, watching John like a teacher waiting for a slow pupil to reach an obvious conclusion, but still being proud of them for managing it on their own.

'If that card had really been torn up whenever it was received, the exposed edges along the tears would have aged as the pieces rattled around in that envelope. They might not be quite as yellow as the rest, but they'd be softened by friction. Instead they still look pretty white compared to the rest. So it was torn up relatively recently. Right?'

'Of course,' Sherlock said, with a pleased smile. John let himself be tugged in to lean against his side in a one-armed hug and tried to keep his own happy expression in check. It was ridiculous how much he enjoyed keeping up with Sherlock's brain.

'The envelope also had a clear outline of the card worn into it,' Sherlock added, 'but very little sign of a bunched up collection of scraps, so it certainly spent more time in there whole than not.'

'But did it actually tell you anything?'

Sherlock leaned forward, pulling John with him, and gently nudged the card to lay flat using the tweezers to protect it from pizza grease. 'Oh, lots.'

The handwriting was faded and old-fashioned, but much of it was still surprisingly legible for a card that had been reduced to such tiny pieces.

> *Dear Mum,*
> *Happy Easter. I hope you, Brian, and the kids are well. I know Brian would rather I not contact you, but I wanted to make sure that you knew I was okay. I found dad. Turns out he had been looking for me. He's sorry he couldn't marry you, but he's glad you found someone. He's married now, too, so I have six half-brothers and sisters. He wanted to do right by me, so he's helped me find a place to live. You don't ever have to worry about me again. I'm going to be fine. If you do ever want to write or visit, my address is below, but I understand if you can't.*
> > *All my love*
> > *Gloria.*

Although Sherlock had done his best, it looked like Gloria's pen had run out when she reached the address.

John could just about make out the *o*, *n* and *n* that was probably 'London', but the rest he couldn't decipher. Fortunately he didn't have to. On the table beside the card was a whole sheet of paper filled with Sherlock's terrible handwriting as he worked through the possibilities.

'You should work in the dead letters office,' John laughed when he saw how easily Sherlock had managed to settle on an address in Wimbledon, south of the river.

Sherlock grinned. 'Who says I haven't?'

Rolling his eyes, John turned his attention back to the card. Other than '1971' written in one corner in a different ink and an older style of handwriting there were no other visible marks on the card.

He looked at the envelope it had been stored in – as Sherlock had said, there was a clear outline of the card worn into the paper but otherwise it was blank.

'No address on the envelope,' John observed after a moment.

'No,' Sherlock agreed. 'I suspect that if this Brian didn't want the daughter to contact the mother then she probably hid the card in something else, a bill perhaps. Something boring that her stepfather wouldn't have noticed.'

John nodded. That made sense in a sad and unjust sort of way.

'The clients did say that Gloria's birth father was a GI: an American soldier,' John said, after a moment. He'd meant to explain all this to Sherlock after the first meeting but he'd forgotten all about it when Sherlock had said he didn't want to take the case. Sherlock might have researched it in the meantime but he sometimes missed the historically significant things. 'Some of them were based in the UK during the Second World War, mostly in rural areas. The locals welcomed them, some people more than others. But, if he wasn't white – and based on her photograph he wasn't – he wouldn't have legally been able to marry her mum because of the American laws at the time. There were a lot of children left without fathers after the war. It looks like in this case the mum's new husband didn't want to adopt someone else's daughter.'

Sherlock looked at him in a way that suggested he was filing away the information, but he didn't ask any follow-up questions. That didn't necessarily mean much when it came to Sherlock.

When it became clear that the conversation had stalled, John prompted, 'so we have a forty-year-old address?'

That didn't seem like much of a lead.

He reached for his third slice of pizza and found it gone. He glared at Sherlock, who handed him the partially eaten slice in his own hand with a shamefaced expression.

'I checked the phone book and she's listed as still living there,' he said with a shrug. 'I've tried the number a few times but no one picks up.'

'What? A phone book? An actual paper phone book? Really?' John was stunned. 'I didn't even know we had one!'

'It's holding up the left hand side of the wardrobe in your room,' Sherlock said. Then he reached out and moved the pizza box to reveal the book in question. 'Well, it was – remind me to put it back before the whole thing tips over. Anyway, I know most people have opted out now, but it can be helpful for finding older people who still want to be listed, or don't know how to opt out. Or who are spies.'

They looked at each other for a moment, John narrowing his eyes suspiciously. He never knew when Sherlock was joking about that sort of thing.

'Very old-fashioned spies,' Sherlock continued. His expression remained unchanged. 'Mycroft's in here, you know.'

He picked it up with greasy fingers and waved the spine towards John as if in demonstration.

'What?' John snatched the book from him and turned to H. 'He never is!'

'Yep, he's not under 'Holmes', though. He's towards the front. Under A.'

John flicked back through the letters. 'What, really?'

'Yep. He's under A.R.S.E.H–' The phone book caught Sherlock a stinging clip to the ear.

'You absolute tit!' John hissed while Sherlock collapsed giggling into the sofa cushions, clutching his ear in mock pain.

'Your face!' he laughed as John's cheeks turned redder.

His day had been too damn stressful for this. 'Right, I'm going to bed!'

'Aww.' Sherlock slumped in place, apparently disappointed that his joke had turned John's good mood sour.

The kicked-puppy act worked on John far too quickly, just like always. He held a hand out towards Sherlock.

'Are you coming or not?'

That, at least, put the smile back on Sherlock's face. It was a tempting sight that John just had to kiss. Even after two years of seeing it every day he couldn't resist.

'You're not working tomorrow, are you?' Sherlock asked, slipping a hand into the waistband of John's trousers as they wove their way toward the bedroom.

'No, the clinic will be shut for a while. Why? Do you want to spend the day in bed?'

John leaned in for another kiss, but found that Sherlock's smile had turned to that annoying look of a detective with a mission.

'There'll be time to stay in bed when we're not on a case, John. We'll just have to make the most of tonight, and then tomorrow we can check out this address.'

'Why do I stay with you?' he asked. He already knew the answer, but on nights like this he wondered if Sherlock really appreciated it.

The kiss he finally received just before Sherlock shoved him toward the bed seemed to suggest that he did.

'Because you love me,' Sherlock said against his lips. 'And I love you, and you love all of this. But mostly because you want to know what happens next.'

Well, John had to laugh, because nothing truer had even been said to him in his life.

CHAPTER FIVE

Present Day – York

BREAKFAST HAD NOT BEEN INCLUDED IN THEIR HOTEL BOOKING.

John hadn't really minded that – he'd eaten his fair share of guest house breakfasts in his time and his arteries would thank him for not consuming a meal consisting entirely of fried meat products – but he had hoped to avoid travelling far for food and 'to the bottom of the staircase' had seemed just about the right distance to him.

Sadly, today was not his lucky day, and so they'd been forced to venture out into the city. Even worse, there had been no kettle in their room – John was facing a search for sustenance without even the benefit of caffeine.

He really needed to cut down.

The street outside the guest house had the quiet, almost deserted feeling of dead-end streets everywhere. No one ventured into that space without a reason. By comparison, the next street was absolutely teeming with that familiar mix of resigned commuters and eager, bumbling tour groups.

He felt almost like they were stepping into the streets of London, but as tourists rather than the self-appointed lord of the city and his faithful companion. There was something freeing in that thought – a kind of egalitarian unfamiliarity that put them on a rare even footing.

Even in medical matters Sherlock was capable of keeping up with John's knowledge if it was relevant to a case, so it was nice to revel in the brief period of equal knowledge before Sherlock inevitably found a map and learned everything there was to know about this tiny city.

Of course, John would have preferred to revel in it on a full stomach.

The first cafe they found was so popular that tourists were queuing out the door. The next inexplicably claimed to be unable to serve them so near to closing time, which from the sign on the door seemed to be three hours away but John was too hungry to argue. The third and fourth sold the kind of artisanal fare that neither of them was desperate enough to stoop to, but the fifth – in the words of Goldilocks – was just right.

John was still chuckling to himself at the image of either of them as the eponymous porridge thief when Sherlock ordered for them both. He decided that Sherlock was the most likely, since he had the lock-picking skills and lack of boundaries necessary for the role, and 'Sherlock' did mean 'bright-hair'.

He was just opening his mouth to explain this odd train of thought – and to wonder out loud if he would ever qualify as a 'bear' – when he realised they were being watched.

They'd taken a tiny two-seater table in a corner. The cafe was so crowded that they were less than six inches from the next table in the row, where a much older man was looking at them with a soft little smile.

The echoes of his dreams the night before made John study his observer in much more detail than was strictly polite, but the man didn't seem to notice. He was too busy acknowledging another customer's apology when she steadied herself on his shoulder as she squeezed by. John felt a little ridiculous for feeling so relieved that the man wasn't a ghost.

'He really knows how to take care of you,' he said suddenly to John in a voice that crackled with age and too many cigarettes. He looked about ninety, but he had that special kind of weather-worn cragginess that made it difficult to tell whether that assessment was fair. His clothes were clean and well-tailored, with a row of medals glittering over his heart like a final flourish on his neatness.

John couldn't even remember where he'd put his own medal.

Blinking in under-caffeinated confusion, he replied 'Pardon?'

'It's good you've found a man who can look after you,' the man said.

To clarify his point he nodded to Sherlock, who had just progressed from assuring the waitress that a three-shot coffee was entirely safe and was now instructing her in the proper way to burn the bacon to John's liking.

The poor waitress wore the glazed expression of many people meeting Sherlock Holmes for the first time, but at least she was writing everything down.

John blushed, oddly pleased to have been pegged as a couple so easily.

'He tries.'

'I don't *try*. If I do something I do it perfectly,' Sherlock said, turning back to the table, having ordered himself a bagel and tea *however it comes*.

John couldn't help laughing at his haughty tone. Sherlock just looked offended, which only made the whole thing funnier.

'If you say so,' John said. The half-hearted attempt to mollify the detective was not successful.

After an appraising glance at the old man, Sherlock turned towards the big windows at the front of the cafe and with a pointed harrumph became instantly engrossed in people-watching.

'Reminds me of my beloved,' the old man chuckled. 'He could never take a joke at that age, either. But then that's war for you.'

John turned in his seat to face him, partially to prove to Sherlock that his sulking was ineffective, but mostly because he was genuinely interested in the man's comments.

He'd met this type before, hundreds of times, on buses and in queues, at memorial services – old men and women with stories to tell whether anyone wanted to listen or not. John had done his best to cultivate a habit of listening to the living while they were still around to be heard. Sherlock would say he rarely understood, but he did try, and really, if the person came away believing that they'd been heard, then that was a success in his book.

Besides, how often did he get to meet older men like himself? So much of the past had been lost in the 80s and 90s – it was only right to hear what history he could.

'You met during the war?'

He had assumed the man meant World War II – he looked to be the age for it – but the man shook his head.

'Korea. We both worked comms. He was in the US Army, I heard his voice for six months before I ever saw his face.' He paused and smiled again, his eyes drifting to the windows with an unfocused look. 'Isn't it strange how people fall in love?'

John looked over at Sherlock, or rather the side of his head, since he was still staring out of the windows, too. He was ever so slightly moving his lips as he followed people with his eyes. Deducing them, maybe.

'At least you got to hear his voice – I fell in love with his music.' John leaned forward then and said in a fake whisper, 'It's hard to remember that when he's playing violin at 4am, though!'

The old man laughed delightedly.

The first time John had heard Sherlock play he'd still been on crutches, and been so distracted by the wonderful music echoing through Tottenham Court tube station that he'd almost fallen off the escalators. It had been a week of hearing him everyday before he actually saw him, and in that moment John had been convinced he was a ghost.

London commuters rarely paid attention to buskers, but this man in an Edwardian frock-coat had seemed far too ethereal to be real. It was only when John stopped someone from stealing his tips – and somehow unwittingly got involved in a case – that he accepted that the beautiful violinist was real.

Some mornings he woke up so in love that he still couldn't quite believe it.

Unless he was rudely awakened, of course. And 4am violin practice was definitely rude by anyone's standards.

Sherlock glanced over with narrowed eyes, which just earned him a friendly tap on the arm.

'As long as he remembers, you can't complain,' the man told Sherlock. He nodded wisely. 'It's when he forgets and throws it out the window that you have to worry.'

'That sounds like the voice of experience,' John laughed.

'I might have had a thing for Elvis, and absolutely no talent for the ukulele.'

The image of a ukulele plummeting towards the street made John snort and cover his mouth. He'd definitely been tempted to take a similar action once or twice.

'But he remembered he loved you in the end?' he asked, once he trusted himself not to laugh again.

At the question the man's face turned a little grim, and John regretted asking. War wasn't kind on anyone, and personnel from different countries rarely ended up being stationed close together more than once. Assuming his boyfriend had survived the war at all.

'Sorry, that was insensitive,' John said quickly, determined to backpedal from the edge of disaster. 'I didn't mean to imply…'

'He did remember eventually, just in time for the start of the new century, in fact,' the man said.

Still without his coffee John's brain failed to follow the comment. 'Sorry?'

'We found each other again through one of those online message boards,' he explained, patting John kindly on the hand as he spoke. 'I figured with the millennium coming up there was nothing left to lose and everything to gain, so I got one of the ladies at the library to help me write a post. Six weeks later he sent me an email and a year after that he moved over here for good. Last Christmas he bought me a new ukulele. He soon regretted it.'

John felt his eyebrows rise in surprise while his mouth opted for a grin of happiness. They'd found each other again after fifty years, then they'd been together for nearly two decades.

The thought filled him with a warm kind of hope that he hadn't felt in a while.

He loved Sherlock, he really did, but at times life got in the way of remembering that. He should try harder.

Sherlock was staring out of the window again, the diffuse light from the steamy cafe windows painting the sharp edges of his profile in silver and gold. Sometimes John felt like there were two Sherlocks – the charming but irascible man who came alive with the chase, and this being who seemed to have stepped straight from a painting, made of music and grace.

Just then the waitress returned, with blessedly strong coffee and a sandwich containing bacon so burnt it was almost charcoal.

When she left again to collect Sherlock's food, a second old man, somehow even more weathered than the first, had settled into the empty seat opposite their new acquaintance. They were talking animatedly, gnarled hands gripping tight across the tabletop like the space around them was their own little world.

Reaching for his fork John let his free hand brush the back of Sherlock's hand.

Sherlock hummed contentedly, and moved his wrist so his hand rested in John's open palm. He didn't turn back from the window this time, barely moving enough to make space for his tea cup when it arrived, but it was enough.

John let his eyes lose focus as he finally raised his first cup of coffee to his lips.

The men at the next table, still in love after all this time, had met, then lost, then found one another all over again.

Sipping his coffee, he thought about the times he'd found Sherlock only to lose track of him again. At least they'd been lucky enough to have only a few weeks between their encounters.

Two Years Ago – Kennington, London

Of course, he would have been entirely justified in refusing the change of appointment time. It wasn't his fault the surgery had double-booked their appointments.

He was a doctor – he knew exactly what effect a lack of therapy could have on his recovery. And if he did refuse then the other patient would just have to wait, though he wasn't even being offered an appointment later that day. They'd tried to put him off for an entire month.

John had been tempted to let the receptionist kick the other man out until he dramatically threw off his coat right there and brandished his arm at her.

He was skinny, far too skinny for John to have considered him attractive, or so he'd thought. Right up until the man flexed his fingers to demonstrate an apparent loss of movement and John saw the most beautiful hands he'd ever seen on a man. He'd looked away immediately in an effort not to imagine what they'd feel like on his skin, but he wasn't all that successful.

'I'm a violinist! Look at the flexion on this! Look!' he shouted.

John had finally looked at him properly then, and was surprised to recognise the face he'd only seen at a distance several weeks before. This was the violinist from Tottenham Court tube station, the one who'd been robbed, then never appeared in the tube station again. Perhaps this injury was the reason why. There was a moment of misplaced guilt when John wondered if he could have done something more to stop the whole situation. The violinist had followed the thief; was this injury a retaliation?

He shook it off – he hadn't nearly enough information to know what had happened there.

As he turned his attention back to the conversation at hand, the receptionist rolled her eyes in a way that made John's military heart want to put her up on a charge. 'Mr Holmes, I simply don't have…'

'He's right, you know,' John cut in, reaching out to almost touch the pale skin with unexpectedly shaking fingers. 'The scar tissue is clearly contracting, he needs to be assessed immediately.'

'Mr Watson–'

'Doctor. Actually. And Captain. I know what I'm talking about, and I'd be happy to speak to this gentleman's solicitors, if anything were to happen as a result of…'

She gave him a look of unadulterated loathing, but at least she picked up the phone this time.

He hadn't actually had any intention of doing anything of the sort, though he could have helped the man find another rehabilitation expert if it was necessary. But he was already sure it wasn't.

There was a certain kind of receptionist who treated the medical staff like they were the crown jewels, hindering patients and practice alike. John had simply wanted to scare her into fetching the owner of the practice. John knew him personally, but a receptionist of this ilk would never believe him.

Gajan had originally trained in the army's rehabilitation program before he'd founded this practice. They knew each other of old – John had sent plenty of patients back to Gajan's tender care, while Gajan had complimented him on keeping as many of them as whole as he could. John knew they could reach an agreement.

What a shame the man had such poor taste in front-line staff. She was already opening her mouth to begin arguing with them again when Gajan appeared from one of the therapy rooms.

'I'm sorry about this, Sherlock,' he said to the violinist before turning to John. 'You know I can't see you both.' His voice was reproachful, but not overly so. He knew John wouldn't be messing him around without reason.

John gave a shrug that was only slightly hindered by his crutches. 'I'm your last appointment before the lunch break. If we overrun I'll buy you lunch all next week.'

'Can you afford that?' Gajan laughed.

'Nope,' John said, with a grin toward the stranger ostentatiously retrieving his coat from the floor. 'So we'd better not overrun, had we?'

Keeping to schedule was easy enough. They only had a half-hour session but John was mostly just repeating his exercises under observation, so Gajan had plenty of opportunity to look over the other man's scars.

It soon became clear that the he was a regular here, and that John's assessment of his condition had been correct. The warm glow he got from that fact certainly made the exercises easier. Or maybe the warmth came from the intensity of the man's gaze.

John had thought he misheard in the waiting room, but the

violinist really did have the unlikely name of 'Sherlock Holmes'. He also had an unnerving way of staring. For some reason Gajan had positioned him facing the bed on which John was lying, and Sherlock seemed physically incapable of looking away. It didn't feel entirely like being eyed up, though. Instead John felt like he was a training cadaver being assessed.

When the room finally fell into silence but for John's slightly pained breathing as he pushed through the leg routine, and the click of Gajan's hands at the computer, Sherlock suddenly said, 'You've been in Afghanistan.'

From the corner of his eye John saw Gajan look up in concern, but John shook his head.

'Ibiza, actually,' he said, holding the other man's gaze. 'I got smashed off my face on MDMA and slipped at a foam party.'

Sherlock's thin lips twitched slightly in what might have been a repressed smile. 'You're a terrible liar.'

'And it seems you're a nosy prick, so I guess that makes us even,' John replied lightly.

'People don't get shot in Ibiza. And they get a better tan than that. I still see the lines where your safety equipment rubbed the sunscreen away.'

John looked down at himself then, just to check whether he was actually wearing the polo shirt he'd put on that morning. There it was, deep burgundy and covering him from neck to mid-bicep. There was no way the man could have seen the bullet wound to his left shoulder. His ruined leg was on display for all to see, but that just looked like the result of a car accident. Which, really, it was.

'How did you know I'd been shot?' he asked, unconsciously rubbing at his shoulder while he spoke.

Sherlock's free hand flicked towards him in an elegant arc as he checked off his reasons. 'Gajan checked your shoulder before setting you to work with your leg; the scars on your leg suggest that a heavy-duty boot took much of the external impact up to a point, but probably contributed to the break itself; you said outside that you were a Captain; and you're wearing a Royal Army Medical Corps shirt.'

'Wow.'

Sherlock grinned ruefully at John's open-mouthed stare. 'Plus, there was an article about an army doctor who was evacuated after bravely saving the life of his patient in a roadside ambush. It mentioned that he had been shot. You seem like the helpful sort.'

'Well,' John said, turning his head to look at the wall in a half-hearted effort to hide his blush, 'you are just a nosy prick, then.'

He let himself smile a little as Sherlock laughed delightedly at the comment but he was still embarrassed at being so taken in by his act.

Sherlock was a stern-looking sort, all hollow cheeks and swept-back hair, but when he laughed there was something purely joyful in the sound that made John want to hear it again. He wondered if the man only came alive through sound. His laughter was almost as perfect as his violin performances.

'Oh! That reminds me!' John said, sitting up and earning himself a look of reproach from the physiotherapist. 'Did you ever get your money back?'

'My money?' Sherlock frowned but didn't seem to understand.

'You were robbed, right? Someone snatched your violin case?'

Suddenly John wasn't nearly as certain of himself as he had been a moment before. Perhaps there were multiple tall, thin, slightly Victorian-looking violinists in London.

'Oh, that…No…I didn't think to look.'

John smiled then, glad to be the bearer of good news for once. 'I was the one who tripped the thief,' he admitted, trying not to puff up too much with pride. 'I didn't manage to save all the money, but I left at least a hundred quid with the station security officers, they probably still have it.'

He felt a little disappointed when Sherlock only nodded thoughtfully at this new information. It wasn't a life-changing amount of money, but it wasn't pocket change, either.

'Seems like you know a lot about me, but I know nothing about you, Mr Holmes. Are you a full-time violinist, or is that more of a hobby?'

'Oh, no,' Sherlock said, wincing a little when Gajan returned to manipulating his arm. 'I tried, but there was a serious artists' disagreement over one or two appointments.'

'You didn't like your colleagues?'

Sherlock sniffed. 'I liked them just fine, but I thought they should be assigned on musical ability rather than aesthetic merits.'

'He was blacklisted for shoving a conductor's baton down his trousers,' Gajan added, with a laugh.

'I merely suggested that if he was going to think with his cock all the time he might as well conduct with it, too. It would probably have done a better job than him at least.'

Sherlock said it so seriously that John couldn't help but howl with laughter at the image. John could just imagine him in that ridiculous Edwardian coat snatching the baton from the conductor's hand. He'd probably waved it in his face, too, before he'd shoved it elsewhere.

'It might have done a better job but it would have been a very strange concert!'

Sherlock nodded. 'A very short one, too.'

'What, the concert? Or the cock-ductor?'

There was a moment where John feared that perhaps he'd gone too far, or the humour of the army didn't entirely translate to civilian life, but then both other men collapsed into fits of giggles.

He grinned, pleased with himself for making others laugh after the last two grim weeks. There'd been a time when he wasn't sure if he'd ever manage that again.

Finally, Gajan wiped his eyes with his sleeve and went back to assessing Sherlock's arm.

'So, what do you do then?' John asked the not-really-a-violinist-anymore. 'Other than pry into other people's lives the instant you meet them?'

There was a snort from Gajan just before Sherlock said, 'Nothing.'

'Professional layabout?'

Sherlock shook his head, his eyelashes flickering in what seemed to be a long-held irritation. 'No, I mean nothing else. I literally pry into people's lives. I'm a detective.'

He didn't look like a policeman, but then John supposed the best detectives didn't these days. Wasn't MI5 always wanting to recruit 'everyman spies'? The Met was probably going the same way.

'Were you injured in the line of duty then? If you don't mind me asking?'

Sherlock frowned a little. 'Sort of. A roof fell on me.'

'I think the fact that you started off *on* the roof is probably relevant to the story,' Gajan added. 'You *caused* a roof to fall on you, by climbing on it.'

'No, two and a half million in misappropriated funds caused the roof to fall on me,' Sherlock corrected. 'And we have enough evidence to prosecute.'

'And a multi-million-pound repair bill.'

Sherlock shrugged despite the grip on his arm. 'Better for me to fall than some ten-year-old on a dare.'

'So you're the helpful sort, too, then,' John said.

Sherlock smiled at him and resolutely ignored Gajan's muttered comment about Sherlock never having helped anyone in his entire life.

He should say something. Anything.

Across the room Sherlock was pulling his shirt back on while Gajan helped John with his shoes. It made him feel more awkward than usual, having someone literally kneeling at his feet to help him with a task he'd mastered at the age of five, and now he couldn't get his voice to work.

He really should say something.

Come on, brain, he thought desperately, he's cute and you love his music, how many chances will you get like this again?

He harangued himself as they walked back to reception in silence, Gajan striding ahead to make sure he never again had another embarrassing scheduling conflict.

Sherlock's hand was inches from his own, the thick fabric of his coat grazing John's crutches with every step. He smelled of attics and flavoured tobacco, an odd mix that made John want to breathe even deeper.

Deep breaths or not, his voice still wouldn't work.

New appointment slots, on different days, at different times.

No chance of an overlap now.

Come on, John…

'Thanks for stepping in,' Sherlock said suddenly, his eyes drifting to study every part of the room but John himself. 'I'm pretty sure she'd have thrown me out if you hadn't interceded.'

John shrugged, the blush that had been loitering around his face for half an hour suddenly back with a vengeance.

'It was the right thing to do. And it…' John swallowed, 'it was a pleasure to meet you at last. I've been listening to your music for a while now. It makes the mornings better.'

The smile Sherlock gave was all teeth and slightly disbelieving eyes. Maybe John could have phrased that better, though he didn't know how.

'Perhaps I'll get to hear you again? At Tottenham Court station?'

'Oh. No, the acoustics there are terrible.' The response was instantaneous, delivered with the blank tone of a poorly-rehearsed script. Just as John's heart began to sink Sherlock continued in a brighter tone. 'King's Cross, though…I always sound much better there. Next week maybe?'

And with that he was gone, all coat and impossibly long stride.

But he was never at King's Cross, not the next week or any other.

John knew that for certain. He'd checked far more often than any sane man should have done.

Present Day – York

Leaving the cafe John was stuck by a sudden sense of discomfort that surprised him.

They'd turned down a narrow side street and the morning

sunlight vanished. John blinked, then instinctively rubbed at his eyes. The buildings around them were small, each little more than an arm's span wide, but they crowded tightly together with barely a passageway between any of them, each storey leaning out a little more towards its counterpart across the pavement. The sky was barely visible above, and the walls to either side of him were almost hidden by hundreds of tourists. Not one of them looked where they were going; they were busy staring up or enjoying the scene through the screens of their mobile phones.

He knew this feeling well from his years in London. The crowds and the noise. But not like this.

There was a layer of claustrophobia here that he hadn't experienced in London, or even in the ancient cities he'd visited during his time in the army.

That feeling was under John's feet, too, narrow lanes of cobbles and old stone that seemed to rise up to trip him every time he found his footing. He was used to the winding back roads of London, but so many of those had been modernised for traffic. York felt like a series of boobytraps, just waiting to knock him on his arse for no better reason than it could.

All the good cheer over breakfast and talking with the old man faded into a glum sort of misery that settled over John's bones like a heavy blanket.

They didn't seem to be going anywhere in particular, and not knowing exactly what Sherlock was up to was beginning to frustrate him. They didn't always share the details of a case while they were in the fray, but the fact that Sherlock had disguised it as a holiday grated on his nerves. Sherlock bullshitted and dissembled far more than any other person John knew. But not about them. Not about important things.

The heavy feeling worsened. He felt cold and strange, as if he were wandering onto the set of a long-abandoned movie and all the people were just projections. Or apparitions.

The woman in their room last night was preying on his mind. John kept finding himself looking at passersby for longer than he should, wondering if they were locals following the paths of daily habit or ghosts unknowingly trapped in a cycle they couldn't break.

They passed a series of bars taking deliveries of beer that blocked the narrow streets and echoed noisily along the old stone walls. Cafes that were oddly quiet despite the scent of coffee, bacon, and cake. Bookshops that tempted Sherlock but disappointed with unknown opening times.

On a good day London woke long before John. Despite the crowds, York didn't seem to wake up at all.

Suddenly Sherlock turned right into a covered alleyway that John had mistaken for no more than a door. He stumbled again, confused by the change of direction and fell directly into Sherlock's arms.

Cold stone at his back, chapped lips against his own, and then they were off again before John had even registered the situation, let alone kissed back.

Stepping out into the sun was like stepping into another reality. There were still tourists here, but they were fewer and more respectful of their surroundings.

In front of them stood a massive medieval hall. Brick at the base, wood and plaster above; an informative sign told him it was the home of a charity that had existed for almost 600 years. Perhaps that was why it was so beautifully cared for and sitting amongst gardens that gave it a sense of living that John hadn't seen in the city up until now. The building was still in use. It was still precious to the same people who'd always cared for it. Except that right now it was also closed to the public.

He stepped forward toward the greenery around the lawns, enjoying the sun on his skin and warmth reflected from the soil.

The city was barely steps away, and yet–

Sherlock was gone.

Less than a minute ago he'd been holding John's arm, now he wasn't anywhere in sight.

John turned slowly, studying his surroundings with the intensity of a man who'd known Sherlock Holmes for two long years. He glanced at the roof of the hall, and the surrounding buildings. He even looked into the patches of shrubbery that were large enough to hide an adult. He walked carefully around the building, peering into shadows and even standing perilously close to the edge of the small river that appeared as if from nowhere along the south edge of the garden. There was no sign of Sherlock.

Returning to the entrance John reread the sign, paying close attention to the opening times. The main hall wouldn't be open for another hour. His eyes followed a painted arrow upward. The door was right there at the top of a short staircase—a heavy dark wooden ironbound thing that no normal person could have opened without a sound.

John opened the supposedly-locked door. Sherlock smiled at him.

'Seriously?'

'I have permission to be in here,' Sherlock said as he turned back to the stack of books under his hands. 'I have a key and everything.'

John sighed. 'I don't believe you.'

Still not looking up Sherlock dug into the pocket of his jeans for a moment before producing a large key on a piece of string.

'The fact that you have a key proves only *that you have a key. .*' John was so close to wagging his finger like an angry school teacher that he wanted to scream in frustration.

He'd had a blessed moment of relaxation in the gardens.

John didn't want to feel like this, he'd much rather live the dream of being a happy couple on their belated honeymoon than slip back into the roles of errant genius and his irritable keeper.

He made a decision. 'I'm going back outside. If you're not outside with me in ten minutes I'm going to... well I don't know where I'm going but I'll go there at speed and you won't find me.'

'You'll be in the cafe up the road with the bottomless pot of tea for £4,' Sherlock replied without looking up. 'You know you will.'

Annoyingly he was right, as usual.

'Oh, fuck you,' John said eloquently. He stomped back outside, letting the door close loudly behind him.

Nine minutes and thirty five seconds later Sherlock stepped through it as silently as a ghost.

John had taken that time to sit in the sun and think. Really think, for once. Whatever Sherlock was doing here there was no urgency to it. They weren't running anywhere, or chasing anyone. They'd strolled to this oddly quiet building.

Could he really ask Sherlock to turn off his mind entirely? Just so he could unwind? Was that really fair? Or was this as close to relaxation as Sherlock was ever going to get?

They were out of London and John had no work pressures to weigh him down. Wasn't that enough?

'Where now?' he asked, resigned to whatever Sherlock had planned for them.

'There's a railway museum across the river,' Sherlock said, with an acknowledging smile. He slipped one hand out of his pocket and intertwined their fingers. 'I thought we might go there.'

'And what exactly is at this museum?'

The look Sherlock gave him seemed to suggest John had lost his mind.

'Trains, John, what do you expect?'

CHAPTER SIX

Three Weeks Ago – Wimbledon, London

JOHN KNEW WHAT HE WAS EXPECTING TO FIND IN THE FLAT ONCE they'd located it, but some superstitious part of his soul didn't want to say it aloud.

He had a menthol-soaked mask in the pocket of his oldest jeans, and he knew Sherlock had a similar object somewhere on his person.

No one had heard from the now-elderly woman in a long time, or seen anyone accessing the flat. They both knew that the mostly likely explanation was that she had already passed on but gone unnoticed. It was rare but it happened.

She certainly wouldn't have been the first corpse that he and Sherlock had uncovered.

Usually they were found once the bills stopped being paid. This case was unusual because, according to a contact at the building management company, all her expenses were being paid for from a trust fund—apparently set up for just that purpose by the mysterious American father who'd been unable to claim her as a child.

Sherlock had managed to wheedle some of the details out of a solicitor at the firm who happened to owe him a favour, but it hadn't helped much. Beyond her initial agreement to the arrangement in the '70s they'd had no further contact with her. From their point of view she could have died only a day later and they would never have known.

Forty years dead or forty days, it would make a difference to the state of the flat. He felt terrible in hoping for the former, though either way dead was dead. Still, he should hope that she'd lived a long and happy life, shouldn't he?

The flat was…odd.

There were letters behind the door, stiff yellowed things, but not as many as he might have expected, given their apparent age. Maybe twenty or thirty at most.

A jacket hung on a hook by the door, the red leather cracked and stiff with age. It had the most impressive shoulder pads he'd ever seen in real life. On the floor teetering red heels lay in a jumble with the sort of tennis shoe his mother used to wear. Keds? Yes, that was it.

John bit his lip and looked towards Sherlock. The other man had pulled a tissue from his pocket and swiped at the row of coat hooks. It came back black with dust.

Beyond the hallway green light shifted as if the sun was being filtered through a forest canopy. The living room was cool but not uncomfortably so. A breeze drifted through the space, setting dust motes dancing through the air.

'Oh, my god,' John whispered, staring towards the windows. 'How could nobody notice that?'

'They've probably forgotten there was ever a flat here.'

Sherlock was probably right. The block of flats had been set into a hillside so that this floor – technically the second – was just below the level of the street that passed this side of the building. No one would be surprised by the thick mass of foliage that had entirely consumed the windows – they would have thought it was just part of the garden.

The building itself dated from the 1920s, and it still had some of the original art deco elements – such as the fragile single-glazed windows. The vines outside had taken advantage of that and almost half the glass was broken so that lilac, honeysuckle, ivy, and even passionflower could crawl across the ceiling with impunity.

Just like the art deco windows had fallen to nature, the rest of the flat's original features had certainly been overwhelmed by the decor. The living room had been painted stark white once to contrast with the glittering black tile floors, and yet more red leather, though this time it was in the form of an oversized sofa sitting opposite a bulky cathode ray television. There was even a Nagel print on the wall.

'I think time forgot this flat was here,' John said.

Sherlock nodded as they moved further into the flat where there was more evidence of the owner's keenly green fingers.

Plant pots crowded every flat surface and hung from the ceiling in stalactites of dusty macramé.

Most of the plants had died long ago and crumbled to dust, though a courageous mint sitting by the kitchen sink had managed to send a runner down the drain and had since taken over half the counter. It smelled fantastic, which really wasn't what John had been expecting.

'One of everything,' Sherlock observed, while he peered into the old Formica kitchen cabinets.

The unexpected sound of his voice across the stillness of the room made John jump, but he managed to push down the gasp that tried to crawl up his throat.

If Sherlock noticed he didn't comment on it. He just opened another cabinet door.

'One bowl, one plate, even one of every kind of glass—not just wine – beer, brandy, whiskey. Clearly alcohol was an interest of hers, but not one to be shared.'

He reached for the small fridge sitting silently under the counter.

'Don't. You. Dare.' John said quickly but firmly. He didn't want to know what kind of smells were contained in a fridge that hadn't been opened in at least a decade. 'It's surprisingly pleasant in this time capsule, please don't ruin it for your own amusement.'

Sherlock rolled his eyes, but left the fridge door blessedly alone.

The bathroom was much the same as the kitchen. There was genuine moss growing in the bathtub. Shelves lined with products John had never heard of, most of them probably banned now for CFCs and other poisons, sat mouldering in the once-damp atmosphere. A dressing gown was draped over the shower rail like it would be retrieved at any moment.

He paused at the last door, waiting for Sherlock to catch up. It would lead to the bedroom. They knew what they were likely to find. They both pulled their scented cloths from their pockets, adding to the smell of mint coming from the kitchen, while Sherlock carefully pushed the door open.

It was hard to see any details through the darkness created by the plants that covered the windows. John reached for his torch, noting the stale but unremarkable air in the room. No windows had been broken here. The flat hadn't been decorated in decades; if she'd lain undiscovered for so long, perhaps there wouldn't be a strong odor any more.

He passed the torch light along the floor first, wondering if she'd fallen but also avoiding the bed for the moment, certain he'd find her there. The room was filled with white furniture, grey under the dust, topped with a frothy excess of peach upholstery. Everything was neat and clean. There was no body on the floor.

John moved the light upward.

There was only a duvet and a blanket printed with a kitschy tiger design folded at the foot of the empty bed.

'It's like she just left,' John said at last, putting both their thoughts into words. He turned to look at Sherlock but he was already crossing to the wardrobes with his own torch in hand. 'I don't think she's…'

A cloud of dust filled the room when Sherlock threw the doors open, but as John predicted there was no body stuffed in amongst the power suits and cocktail dresses.

Still, the detective stood with his head on one side, studying the clothes.

'What?'

'These weren't being worn,' Sherlock said, gesturing to the left side of the wardrobe where the more formal clothing sat.

'Sherlock, no one's been in here in…'

He had his back turned to John but Sherlock definitely rolled his eyes again.

'I meant – wherever and whenever she went, in the run-up to that moment she was only wearing the clothes at this end.' Again he pointed. 'See? These are all hanging straight and tightly compacted. I think they were ironed, put away carefully, and then forgotten. These few, on the other hand, were handled more. They're not so neat, like they were pulled out often.'

John moved to stand next to him. He tried to see what Sherlock saw in the arrangement of clothes, but it wasn't nearly as clear to him. It never was. But he did at least see the difference in the clothes in question.

'The stuff on the left is all formal – more structure, stiffer fabrics. Work wear. Evening wear.'

Sherlock nodded. 'And these are soft. Jersey and cotton weaves. Loose fitting.' He blinked. 'We should look through her documents.'

It was John who found the explanation for the clothes, surprisingly in the eighth letter out of the pile of envelopes he'd picked up from the doormat.

The first few were relatively recent letters from the heir hunting agency, but this was much older and bore the return address of a hospital he'd never heard of before.

'Sherlock, look,' he said as he held the letter out for inspection, knowing Sherlock would want to open it himself. 'Acute Oncology Services. I think she had cancer.'

The envelope received the usual minute examination before it was opened with the delicacy befitting its age. There was a stiff mildewed quality to the paper that seemed to prove it hadn't been moved in years.

Sherlock read it once then passed it back.

'Just as I'd thought,' he said, 'she had a sudden lifestyle change. You can see it in the clothes – comfort became a priority. It's in the bathroom products too. There's a lot of half-used bottles pushed to the back in favour of things with 'gentle' in the name. I can't imagine they did much good in 1983, but she did what she could. Old bottles of vitamins and other health supplements in the kitchen too.'

John studied the contents of the letter himself, trying to roll his medical knowledge back to a time when he'd barely been able to read.

'This is treatable. Now. Usually it's caught in time, there's better testing, more accurate treatment. In those days, though…' He sighed, wondering how much pain she'd been in.

Even in this state, with nature trying to reclaim the dated furnishing, the flat held so much personality it made him sad to think its owner was gone. He'd known she was dead before they'd even opened the door – he'd been certain of that. But he'd thought they'd find that she'd died anonymous at a ripe old age. He hadn't expected to feel this level of connection to a woman who'd likely died before her 40th birthday.

They'd handled murder cases in the past and he'd never felt like this before.

As both a doctor and a soldier he dealt with the dead and dying more times than he could count, but somehow this was different. There was an energy to the flat he couldn't put his finger on. Something about the calm quiet of it. The sensation bothered him.

'Could she have recov–'

'No.' John cut him off quietly. 'Stage 4. Even now for this cancer it's…no. She wouldn't have lived much past a year after this letter.'

Sherlock hummed, and turned back to sifting through the rest of her papers.

'Did you hear me? She's dead.'

He didn't know why this situation was upsetting him so much, but suddenly the sight of Sherlock digging through the remains of her life made him sick to his stomach.

No one had noticed she was gone. She'd had six half-siblings and no one had noticed she was gone until they wanted to make sure she didn't get a share of their money.

The realisation hit him like a blow to the chest.

That was it.

If he hadn't met Sherlock.

If that one chance encounter of a double-booked appointment hadn't happened. If he'd just stepped aside and let Sherlock take the appointment for himself. If he'd walked away... Would he have ended up this alone? This forgotten?

Would someone have been breaking into that borrowed flat, months after he... He stopped that thought in its tracks. His PTSD, his depression, they'd never been so bad that he would have...

No. They had been that bad. He'd been convinced then that no one would even have noticed if he died, and this, this could have been him, it could have been his ending, this sad, empty...

He was enveloped in warmth. Sherlock was crouching by his chair, that long fine nose buried in his hair, musician's hands kneading gently at his shoulders.

'You're not dead.'

'I know.'

'You're not alone and I'll never let you be alone.'

'I know.'

'This isn't you.' Sherlock was speaking low and calm and soft. Every word fluttered through John's hair like a caress. It eased the racing he hadn't even noticed in his chest.

'What happened here was sad. But we still don't know where she is. As much as I think the original case is some kind of scam or tax dodge or something I haven't worked out yet, I don't like leaving mysteries unsolved. Yes, from what that letter says – she'd dead. But she never read it. We don't know if she ever received that news. We don't know why she left or where she went.'

John sighed and let go of the tension in his limbs. His leg and shoulder ached, and his head was throbbing. He just wanted to leave this weird time capsule and get back to reality.

'Sherlock, it's been thirty years. We're not going to find anything. As nice as that might be. Where the hell would we even find any leads?'

He watched Sherlock gesture around the flat with a rising sense of claustrophobia.

'No.' He shook his head emphatically. 'No, I can't stay in here. I'm going home. You can stay if you like and look for lost causes but I'm going home.'

'John, I need to find enough evidence for plausible proof of death or the estate won't be paid out.' Sherlock said, squeezing John's shoulders again as if he could make him stay in place. They both knew John wouldn't stay anywhere he didn't want to, not without good reason.

'This hospital was torn down in the late '90s, I have no idea whether her records would have been transported anywhere or just destroyed. Without a body...'

Sherlock stopped at the hand pressed over his mouth.

'I'm going home,' John repeated. 'But I'll call all of our contacts. She didn't die here. If she collapsed and died somewhere in the city there's probably a police or morgue record of an unknown woman fitting the right age and description. If there was an autopsy there'll be a record of the cancer, too.'

He stood awkwardly from the table, his leg stiff from too long spent under tension. 'I'm not going to be useless, Sherlock, but I'm not going to be here.'

He was most of the way out of the door when he heard Sherlock say, 'You're never useless, John.'

Some days he just couldn't believe that.

CHAPTER SEVEN

Two Years Ago – City of Westminster, London

THE CAFE WAS AS QUIET AS ANY PUBLIC SPACE IN CENTRAL LONDON COULD be on a sunny Friday afternoon. Which was to say the place was absolutely heaving. Usually he liked it that way.

Today there was a bubble of quiet around John that he couldn't entirely explain. Perhaps it was his appearance – he hadn't shaved in a few days and his hair was getting long – or maybe it was just the air of gloom around him. He felt so miserable this morning that he could almost imagine a cartoon storm cloud floating over his head.

Of course, the quiet didn't last for long, but then it never did.

'Hello, you!' The voice was bright and affectionate, and completely unfamiliar to him.

He'd had a bad night. A week of bad nights, really, culminating in a night of such intense cramp that he'd half expected to vomit from the pain. He really didn't feel like being subjected to unnecessary enthusiasm. If this was some proselytising religious lunatic then he was going to give him a piece of his mind.

John glanced up from his extra strong black coffee with eyes that were far, far too worn out for cheerful people right now.

Standing beside his tiny table in the cafe's window was the violinist. He stood casually, fingertips resting on the tabletop to support his weight as he smiled down with a look that was half manic. The long Edwardian coat was gone in deference to the spring warmth outside. It had been replaced with a tweed waistcoat that had seen better days but still fitted in a way that made John's mouth turn dry.

Whatever John had intended to say in response to the rude

interruption of his solitude died in his throat, leaving him to sit with his jaw hanging open like a stranded fish.

Which was how the violinist's tongue ended up in his mouth so easily when the man ducked down to press a passionate kiss to his lips.

Since his brain was unable to process the situation enough to issue orders, John's hands unilaterally decided to run through the long, gelled hair, while his tongue decided to follow the interloper's example and kiss back. His body seemed to enjoy it – adrenaline flooding through his system and a contented hum rising in his throat – even if his mind continued to flail at this unexpected turn of events.

Sherlock – some part of his memory recovered enough to supply that detail from their encounter at the physiotherapy office – tasted like sugar with a hint of cigarette. John had always scoffed at the overly romantic notion of associating a person with particular scents and tastes, but even after two months the smell of old books and wet wool had been just strong enough the first time they met to leave an impression on him.

Much to his embarrassment, John's libido came online first, wondering loudly what Sherlock might smell like under all that fabric. He breathed deeply through his nose, chasing that underlying scent, but the quiet noise was just enough to break the spell.

He gasped at the chill in Sherlock's fingers against his cheekbones as the man eased back just enough to whisper against his lips between gentle pecking kisses.

'Good man. Play along, it's important.' So Sherlock really was a…what was it? A spy? A detective? Yes, that sounded right.

Of course he'd known, on a rational level, that someone he'd only managed to speak to once wouldn't be kissing him like a lovesick paramour on their second encounter, but he had to admit that he was a little disappointed. Still, that was no reason not to put some effort into the role.

He leaned into the kiss, chasing Sherlock's lips while he let his body be rearranged just so.

Suddenly the contact cut off with a breathless laugh.

'Sorry, darling, I just couldn't resist,' Sherlock said at a normal volume. He sank into the chair opposite John at an angle that would be interpreted as casual to anyone who hadn't noticed him turning John this way and that.

Clearly Sherlock wanted to watch someone sitting behind John.

'It's only been twelve hours, but you're acting like you haven't seen me for weeks,' John replied with a smile of his own, happy to improvise some kind of conversation. This was the most interesting thing that had happened to him in months. Since he'd stopped that thief in the tube station, in fact.

Sherlock let his brows rise in a look of puppy-like sadness. 'You know I hate it when you have to work nights.'

'You knew the nature of the job when you proposed,' John said, taking the hand Sherlock was resting on the table in his own. 'You can't expect me to change that now.'

Again cold fingers stroked across his cheek. 'I just wish you could get more sleep.'

A chair squeaked across the tiles behind him.

There was a squeeze of his hand, almost too subtle to notice, if he hadn't been expecting something like it.

John smiled and looked away almost shyly, noting the man in the tweed jacket and burgundy trousers heading towards the door. He followed him with his eyes while he replied, 'Perhaps you should switch to the night shift, too, then you could keep me company, I sleep better when you're there.'

The door of the cafe chimed as the man passed through it.

He could feel himself blushing at the fond look Sherlock gave him in return, and leant forward to hide his reaction with another kiss. 'He turned right into St James's Street.'

Leaning back, he said, louder, 'You'd better get back to work, you don't want to be late.'

He'd barely finished the sentence before Sherlock was gone again.

The blush was still burning in his cheeks when he glanced down at his half-empty cup. He saw the future stretching out in front of him like coffee grounds could stand in for tea leaves. Lonely mornings in bustling cafes without another soul to talk to; lonely journeys to medical appointments without any decent reason to heal. Loneliness. Hopelessness. Monotony.

Eight and a half million people in London. What were the chances of running into this same mysterious man twice?

John threw back the last bitter dregs of his drink and headed for the door.

Was he thinking clearly? Of course not.

Did he care? Not in the slightest.

If he'd stopped to consider the matter he would have realised that he didn't know where the man was going, or what Sherlock was intending to do. He would also have realised that with his leg there was no way he could possibly keep up with either of them.

Fortunately, it seemed he'd lost his taste for clear thinking when he first heard the music at Tottenham Court station.

Instead of following Sherlock and his target, John turned in the opposite direction and quickly headed into Green Park. The wide path through the trees was heaving with tourists, if not quite as busy as St James's Street. He could cope with weaving between meandering packs of sightseers – though he did have to dodge one or two bicycle couriers – but he'd walked for hours here during his initial recovery, and he knew ways that were a little less obvious to the casual visitor.

It was an obvious choice for a well-dressed criminal, though.

John was just passing Spencer House when he stepped left out of the crowd and into a wrought-iron lined alley that widened only slightly into the end of Cleveland Row. Not far away, peeking dull red and not all that imposing amongst the tall white Georgian town houses, was the front of St James's Palace itself with its armed police guard.

He paused and pretended to adjust his crutches.

A disreputable-looking criminal would try to avoid the police, but the man from the cafe had looked just like any one of the local wealthy homeowners, and he'd been walking at a normal pace. He was probably expecting Sherlock to turn left onto Pall

Mall while he could just nod to the police as he sauntered away into the open space of the park.

John was right.

Tweed jacket flapping behind him, the target appeared around the corner from St James's Street. No one was behind him.

From the corner of his eye John saw the man actually wave at the nearest officer, a portly man who was practically resting his MP5 on the swell of his stomach. The officer didn't respond, though at this angle John couldn't tell if he was looking elsewhere or not.

Well, now he was at the end of a narrow street blocking the only exit, without any clue about what he was going to do and no sign of Sherlock anywhere.

Sherlock hadn't even asked him to help after the cafe.

What if he was just following the man as part of some bigger case? What if he wasn't the target at all and Sherlock was supposed to be protecting him? What if Sherlock was really a criminal himself and he'd just fooled John's physiotherapist into believing something else?

What the hell was John doing?

The man was barely fifteen feet away now.

Having run out of things to do with his crutches John pulled out his phone and opened his text messages. It was easy to look nonchalant with a phone in one's hand. Perhaps staring blankly at three dozen appointment reminders would inspire some plan of action.

Just as he moved his thumb to scroll back the phone rang.

That would have made him jump at the best of times, but keyed up as he was John practically levitated at the unexpected noise.

The phone flew from his hand.

Reaching out to catch it he dislodged the crutches that had been leaning against his hip.

They fell as if in slow motion to clatter onto the ground directly in front of the target's feet, and in his turn the man was too surprised to avoid them.

For the second time John came to Sherlock's aid by tripping someone with his crutches.

The situation was utterly ridiculous. John would have laughed if Sherlock hadn't suddenly appeared beside him, having dropped down from the scaffolding above.

This time John's phone didn't survive the fright, but it did at least bounce off the face of the man struggling to get up from the ground before it smashed against the kerb.

The man stopped struggling and collapsed, knocked out cold.

John looked from the figure at his feet, to Sherlock, and then to the police officer walking quickly toward them with his gun held a little less casually than before. Years of experience in crisis management took immediate control of his tongue.

'Uh, well, the good news is that I'm a doctor,' he said to the approaching officer in as reassuring a tone as he could manage, 'but I still think you'll need to call an ambulance.'

How he was going to explain Sherlock's presence he had no idea, but as it turned out that wasn't necessary. Apparently everyone at the Met knew his strange new acquaintance.

Despite the sergeant's assurance that everything was fine, and the surprisingly good tea he'd been given to help him 'calm down', John couldn't help but feel unnerved about the entire situation. Sherlock's unblinking stare really didn't help.

He hadn't thought things through in the slightest. He knew he hadn't considered his actions before he took them. But really, would anyone think that tripping someone with their crutches would lead to being interrogated by...who? Interpol? He really wasn't sure.

At best, John had assumed that he'd be helping Sherlock intercept some petty criminal – a thief like in the tube station, or a fraudster, perhaps. So far he had no idea who he'd knocked unconscious, but every few minutes serious men in serious suits would peer around the doorframe at him like he was some kind of curiosity.

The interrogation itself hadn't been that bad, although it had been sort of humiliating.

How long had he been working with Sherlock? Why had he got involved if he'd only met the man twice before? Was he sure he'd been given no instructions? Seriously, what was he thinking?

He'd tried to be circumspect. He'd tried to keep his dignity and pretend that he had thought with his brain and not some other part of his anatomy, but Sherlock had just sat there next to the interviewing officer with a curious look on his face until John had snapped.

John had snapped that being kissed by a gorgeous man had entirely robbed him of his reason. He'd admitted that he'd got himself involved in whatever this was just because he had nothing better to do and he desperately wanted to see Sherlock again.

The officer had given him a look of such gleeful understanding that John had wished for the ground to open up beneath his feet.

Now it was just the two of them sitting in uncomfortable silence, John staring into his tea while Sherlock apparently tried to stare into his soul. There were no windows, and no clock in this tiny room, not that John could see at least, and with his phone now in pieces in an evidence bag somewhere he couldn't really guess at the time. It felt like a million years had passed, but that was probably an overestimation. Probably.

Another ice age crawled by and John suddenly found that he couldn't stand the silence any longer.

'Are you going to tell me what's going on?' he asked, eyes still fixed on the paper cup because something in his brain was telling him he'd catch fire if he looked directly into the other man's intense stare.

'Nope.'

'Helpful.'

'I'm not ungrateful,' Sherlock said in a tone that really didn't sound all that convincing, 'I'm just confused.'

'*You're* confused?'

Sherlock finally looked away from him, crossing his arms and leaning back in his chair as if he was contemplating all the secrets of the universe, not just some retired army doctor with more time on his hands than he had common sense.

'You were telling the truth, about your reasons for following me.'

'Yes, because this is a police station and it's generally the best policy of the innocent to tell the truth, especially if they've done nothing wrong and have no idea why the fuck they're here.' John cut himself off then. He knew his voice was rising from frustration but he had no wish to embarrass himself even further.

'Why didn't you, uh,' Sherlock faltered and John was surprised to see he was actually blushing, 'why didn't you say something the first time we met?'

'I rather thought I did, but you seemed just as embarrassed as you do now. I'm sorry, I know following you probably creeped you out…' John could tell he was blushing now as well, and decided to take the plunge in another moment of inadvisable madness. 'But you kiss so well that I sort of lost my reason.'

He regretted the words as soon as they fell from his lips but there was nothing he could do to take them back. Sherlock had no doubt kissed him as just another part of his cover for whatever this case really was, and now John was adding to his discomfort by admitting that he'd enjoyed it.

Before Sherlock could comment any further the door creaked open and this time the people who had been peering at them actually sat down.

John was forever ashamed to admit that he didn't understand the conversation that had followed.

He had tried, he really had, but between exhaustion and the lingering embarrassment of admitting that he'd liked Sherlock's attention he was already at a disadvantage. Add to that the fact that the mysterious agency representatives still seemed to disbelieve his repeated assertion that he knew nothing about the case, and frankly everyone else in the room might as well have been talking in code.

Sherlock had nodded along as if the entire situation had made complete sense, and somehow John was unwilling to embarrass himself further by admitting that he didn't understand.

Which was how he found himself accidentally agreeing to move into Sherlock's spare room.

He replayed the conversation in his head on the uncomfortable taxi ride from station to flat but he still couldn't see how or why it had happened. Everyone in the room had just agreed that it was for the best. Why was a mystery he couldn't tease apart.

Still, however impulsive he might have been earlier in the day, he had at least recovered his good sense enough to know that he shouldn't question it in front of the taxi driver. Whatever the case involved it seemed to have high enough stakes to warrant a 'trust no one' approach.

Then he'd been compelled to make small talk with the landlady while Sherlock vanished with the supposed aim of making his flat fit for visitors. 'Supposed' because when John finally went to look for him, after an hour's absence, he found a living room that looked like a tornado had passed through it and a kitchen that would probably benefit from the cleansing touch of a house fire or two. If Sherlock had done anything towards tidying up he'd not got far before he'd been distracted by one of the tottering stacks of paper that took up much of the floor.

The landlady followed him into the flat where she stood complaining about the state of it until a plainclothed police officer arrived with a bag of John's belongings. That was something he didn't remember authorising but was still too embarrassed to question.

At least the arrival of his clothes seemed to remind Sherlock of his duties as a host. John had been chivied upstairs to a dusty room that was at least blessedly free of the explosion of papers that carpeted the main floor of the flat, even if it also lacked all but the most basic of furnishing. There was a single bed with a duvet so thin it might have been a sheet and what seemed to be a rock masquerading as a pillow. There wasn't even anywhere to actually put away his clothes.

And there he had been left, without explanation or even an opportunity to ask for one.

All he got was a hasty 'this is your room, good night' before Sherlock vanished.

For three weeks.

On the whole that one eventful day rather set the scene for the next few years of his life.

CHAPTER EIGHT

Three Weeks Ago – Marylebone, London

JOHN WAS DOZING IN ONE OF THE ARMCHAIRS WHEN SHERLOCK RETURNED from Gloria's flat in the early hours of the morning.

He had a very '80s duffel bag slung over one shoulder, emitting a heavy smell of dust, old books, and…fresh bread?

'I didn't find anything else of much interest in her papers,' Sherlock said, as soon as he entered the room. As he spoke he pulled packages from the bag and distributed them along the coffee table. 'I found the name of a doctor with an online obituary from the early noughties, and several nurses I haven't been able to trace yet. There's a small chance they might remember her if they're still alive.'

'There were no unidentified bodies matching Gloria's description found anywhere in London in the decade following that diagnosis letter,' John said sleepily. 'I've emailed other police forces but without the sort of links we have with the Met I can't be sure we'll get a speedy or accurate response.'

Sherlock hummed his thanks and held out a paper bag.

'What's this?'

'I walked back past Giancarlo's place,' Sherlock said, naming a local specialist bakery. 'He's finally got the insurance payout from that fire we investigated for him, so he decided to show his gratitude in an edible format.'

John bit into the roll. It was hot and fluffy and stuffed with diced sausage.

'Holy shit, this is amazing,' he mumbled around another mouthful. 'I could get used to being paid like this.'

'With a mouthful of sausage? I can arrange that.'

He tried to laugh but almost choked. 'You're an arse.'

Sherlock held out another bag with a grin. 'He also paid us in money too.'

That, at least, was a relief. John had had no leads on suitable work since the walk-in centre was forced to close, and he was beginning to worry that he'd have to take on some A&E shifts. Mrs Hudson never hassled them for the rent but somehow that just made him feel even more guilty about being later than they had to be with it.

'What's the rest of this then?' John asked. He leant forward to inspect the duffel bag with his free hand. He winced when his leg protested at the abrupt movement after so long in the same position.

Stooping slightly to slip his fingers into the cuff of John's jeans, Sherlock ran a cool, soothing hand over his scars.

It felt wonderful.

Sherlock had spent hours, once, when they were still so new to one another, mapping the contours of John's wounds. He'd learned the tender places, the places where the damaged nerves always screamed, and the places where they were dead. He'd learned which muscles became tense with overuse and which ached with the rain.

Then he'd systematically tried to work out how to relieve all those problems.

His hands felt amazing even if they weren't always effective. John still needed to rest, and he had to be relatively relaxed, but more often than not it helped. Even on the days when the pain refused to lessen it was still calming to feel Sherlock's hands on him for no other reason than to give comfort. On hard nights, when the dreams kept him awake, it might be the only thing that made John feel human.

Slowly John realised that Sherlock was still holding out a package towards him with a fond little smile.

'Sorry,' he muttered. 'You know how that gets me.'

The package contained a thick blue notebook of the kind more commonly used by school children than adults. There was a tag carefully attached to it with details of where it was found written in Sherlock's terrible handwriting.

'Diaries. Thirty of them.' Sherlock explained. 'It seems that Gloria liked to write about every aspect of her life. I think it might still be worth reading through all of them but this looks to have been the final one.'

John stuffed the last of the bread roll into his mouth and brushed his hand against his jeans before he opened the book. This didn't seem to be a criminal case, and the subject was almost certainly long since dead, but John still felt uneasy about sullying her possessions with floury fingerprints.

Sherlock was certainly right about Gloria's habit of writing about everything. A quick scan of the first few pages showed that she gave equal importance to the weather and her neighbours' habits as to her work concerns and romantic attachments. She seemed to have been a popular woman, given the sheer number of social events she was invited to, and even more touching was the fact that she rarely had anything bad to say of anyone. Within twenty pages John saw her forgive two different men for breaking her heart, and she even spoke of willingly giving money to a girl who'd tried to steal her handbag at knife point.

Apparently, Gloria had been a cheerful sort who rarely gave in to melancholy, even though it was instantly clear to John that she had been a very unwell woman.

At the end of every entry – crammed into a single line almost like an afterthought – was a list of words.

'Have you noticed this?' he asked Sherlock, and read one such line out loud. '*Nausea, AM. Stairs too much. No dinner. Short breath. Bleeding. Sleep 3 hours.* She spent three paragraphs talking about the bin men arguing in the street but her own symptoms read like the shipping forecast. Huh, the next one has blood test results written in shorthand, too.'

Sherlock made a gesture that might have been a shrug. He'd folded himself onto the floor at John's feet in such a way that John couldn't see much more than the top of his head, though he could feel his movements through the hand still resting delicately on his ankle.

'Perhaps she wanted to track her symptoms without dwelling on them?'

John nodded, thinking of the discreet tracker app on his own phone. 'She never even mentions getting bloods drawn. We know when she went to the corner shop for some milk but not when she went to the hospital.'

'Can you tell how far the disease had progressed?'

'Not yet.'

Silence filled the room but for the turning of pages and Sherlock's occasional frantic scribbling as he leafed through the earlier volumes.

John wasn't sure what Sherlock might have found of interest but for every page he turned with his own hands John could see that both Gloria's handwriting and the length of her diary entries was deteriorating.

Where before the events in her office might have taken up half a page, the matter of her retiring on the grounds of ill health warranted barely a complete sentence. For the most part the entries stopped talking of other people and events beyond the balcony of her flat. She spoke more of the birds she fed at the railing now than she did anything else.

Except that once a week, perhaps as a result of treatment she was receiving but still not talking about, the diary went on long rambling asides about, well, more or less anything. Here were two pages about the best sunset she'd ever seen; a three page description of Aachen cathedral complete with sketches and diagrams; a pencil drawing labelled 'I & J' that showed two children staring intently at something just out of view; a list of all the beaches she'd ever visited and her favourite things about each one; an essay on the language of flowers; a written portrait of a beautiful woman Gloria had known as a teenager.

The only thing the entries had in common, other than being undated, was the fact that each and every one of them was positive. Even the pages where she spoke of her parents spun all the difficulties into an advantage. The way people had treated her single mother had taught her to be kind; struggling for food taught her to be generous, etc.

Maybe she'd been advised to use writing as some kind of therapeutic technique. John wondered if it had helped. He'd never been able to concentrate on that kind of thing, and even reading her words was wearing him out. For all the positivity on the page John found himself feeling nothing but sadness.

The last page revealed something that he was surprised Sherlock hadn't spotted, though perhaps he just hadn't mentioned it.

'This isn't Gloria's final diary,' John said as he gently tossed it onto the coffee table next to Sherlock's hand.

Sherlock twisted around to look at him with one of his annoyingly blank expressions.

'People don't conveniently fill up an entire diary to the very last page before they die,' John explained, 'and no one who wrote every single day would think *I'm going to die so I might as well stop now this one is full.*'

There was still no response from Sherlock.

John poked him in the ear with a toe.

'It does seem like too convenient a stopping point, doesn't it?' he finally replied. 'The date is a few months before the letter we found unopened on the doormat, and I looked in the fridge after you left–'

'Delightful,' John said, his throat constricting at just the thought of what that must have smelled like after all those years to fester.

'Surprisingly it was,' Sherlock laughed. 'The fridge was empty.'

'Really?'

Sherlock hummed in an oddly satisfied way as he nodded.

So the flat hadn't been abandoned suddenly after all. Someone must have emptied out the fridge at some point.

'The only thing left in there was a thin layer of cardboard packaging that must have stuck to the ice when the freezer section was still running.'

Sherlock showed him a sealed plastic pouch with a sliver of paper inside. The paper was yellow and the print was worn but the design was recognisable as a once-popular ice cream brand.

'I'd have to contact the company,' Sherlock continued, 'to establish what year that design is from, but from the aesthetics…' He shrugged and turned to another book from the pile he was browsing through.

John nodded, there was definitely an '80s vibe to what he could see of the design.

'So the fridge was emptied and turned off but not actually cleaned?' he asked. 'If it had been cleaned that bit of paper would have been destroyed, surely.'

'Yup.' Sherlock nodded so his head brushed John's knee. The contact was enough to tempt John into running his fingers through the soft hair at the nape of his neck where the gel had worn away. 'There wasn't much other food left behind in the cupboards, just a few cans with long past use-by dates. That'd explain the lack of rodent activity, at least.'

There wasn't much John could say in response to that, so he didn't bother. At this early hour he didn't want to think about anything but going to bed. Instead he let the fingers in Sherlock's hair dip below his collar in the hope of giving him a hint.

The hope that Sherlock would take a hint was, as always, unfounded.

Although Sherlock settled back a little to give John better access to his skin he didn't stop his task of sorting through the books, so in the end John rearranged himself until he was laid in the chair with his head resting on the arm.

From there he could watch Sherlock's profile and the movement of his quick, clever hands. But given the hour, it was no surprise that Sherlock's movements lulled him to sleep.

John woke to find himself being *carried* – inexpertly and with a lot of whispered swearing – but carried nonetheless to bed. Given the fretting of his carrier John decided to pretend he was still asleep, more to avoid being dropped in surprise than for any other reason.

Though he had to admit that he did enjoy the rare sensation of being in someone else's arms.

Despite his thin frame Sherlock was surprisingly strong, all wiry muscles combined with a stubborn kind of determination. Even so he hadn't done *this* since their wedding day, and on that occasion he'd only carried John three steps over the threshold of the flat before they'd ended up fucking on the floor. John felt his cock twitch at the thought and bit his lip. That had been a good day.

'I know you're awake, you know,' Sherlock griped as he shuffled sideways through the bedroom door. John's feet caught on the frame making him hiss in pain. 'Sorry.' The apology didn't sound all that sincere.

John opened his eyes to glare at him, but the soft kiss he received wiped the idea from his mind. For just a moment John saw the pale yellow glow of dawn just visible around the curtains before he was dropped unceremoniously onto the bed and his vision was instantly obscured by Sherlock flopping down on top of him.

'Oof. Watch it or you'll crush me,' he said, shoving halfheartedly at Sherlock's shoulder.

The protest earned him nothing but a flex of the hips resting over his own. John caught them in a firm grip and leaned up to kiss the mouth that had just opened to complain at the limitation of Sherlock's movements.

'Not right now,' John said, as gently as he could.

Sherlock pouted slightly, but still rolled away to haul the blankets up over them both.

'You're definitely not working today?' Sherlock asked the question almost like it was an order.

'No. The walk-in centre is still closed and I haven't heard anything from the agency yet,' John admitted. Now that he was free of Sherlock's weight he rolled onto his side, then shuffled forward until their knees slotted neatly together.

'Good.'

Sherlock took his hand but didn't say anything else.

'What now? For the case, I mean.' Although sleep was lurking at the edge of John's senses, he knew he wouldn't settle without at least a vague idea about the next steps.

At first he thought Sherlock had fallen asleep because he couldn't hear anything but slow breathing from the other side of the bed, but just as he started to drift off he heard Sherlock mutter, 'Nothing. It's finished.'

'What? You solved it?'

That didn't sound right. Sherlock hadn't had his usual smug delight when he brought John in here, and John refused to believe that tucking him into bed would ever take precedence over celebrating the great detective's brilliant mind.

'No. I don't think there's anything to solve. A sick woman went away. You said yourself that she wouldn't have lived long with that kind of cancer. A record of her body will turn up somewhere, we just need to wait for the regional record keepers to get back to us.'

Sherlock paused and shifted slightly so he could drape his free arm over John's hip. 'I already emailed the clients with details of the treatment she was receiving, hopefully that will help them get a declaration of presumed death.'

John nodded against the pillow.

Such a certificate would normally be issued if seven years had passed after someone was likely to have died. In this case they knew that Gloria had been suffering from an advanced form of cancer that would have been unsurvivable in the early '80s. The minimum time frame had definitely passed since then.

'Good,' he said, without entirely meaning it. 'It was getting ghoulish, just digging through all her things with no suspicion of wrongdoing. It felt like a sacrilege.'

There was a strange noise from the other side of the bed, but if Sherlock had any thoughts on that he kept them to himself. Still, this was an unexpected change of heart on Sherlock's part. Usually he wanted to see things through to the end, and he'd been enthusiastic about the investigation only a few hours before.

Suddenly John realised something that should probably have occurred to him earlier.

'What about her will?' he asked. 'Did you find anything? Any mention of a solicitor?'

If Ian and Jessica – the clients who'd hired them for this case – were close enough relations to Gloria to share an inheritance, wasn't there a chance that they'd inherit Gloria's estate as well?

John couldn't explain why he felt so defensive of this woman he'd never met, but those two really didn't seem like the sort of people who deserved to get her things. Would they appreciate what they were getting? Some of the essays in that last diary were good enough to publish – would they care about that or would they just see pound signs when they took ownership of the flat?

'That's not our job, John,' Sherlock said in a tone that was far more gentle than was usual for him. 'That's for the heir hunters to find out now. We just needed to prove she was gone.'

John sighed. This was what he'd wanted, so why did it feel wrong?

He didn't have the energy to question it any more. This was Sherlock's case. Not his. He was just along for the ride, as always.

He closed his eyes and focused on the steady sound of Sherlock's breathing.

Outside the window London was waking up again but they weren't going to join the hustle and bustle of daily life. That wasn't who they were today. No doubt in an hour or two someone would come thundering up the stairs to demand Sherlock's attention, and then the two of them would be running again. But for now they were just two men sleeping side by side and John was going to make the most of it.

'John?' Sherlock whispered so quietly that he could have pretended not to hear him if he wanted. 'Are you awake?'

'No.'

A gust of soft laughter made his hair flutter against his skin. 'I love you. We never got our honeymoon. Maybe we could, I don't know, go away sometime soon?'

Sherlock was rubbing slow circles over John's hip with his fingertips, the rough calluses from years of violin practice scratching with just enough force to feel soothing. Almost soothing enough to distract John from the realities of the question.

They were not the sort of men to take holidays.

John frowned in the dark. 'Can we afford it?'

'We still have the honeymoon fund.'

'Really?' That was news to him. 'Then why did we go without a washing machine for two months if we had money lying around?'

'Be reasonable, John,' Sherlock said. 'A washing machine is not a honeymoon.'

John did his best to muffle a scream of frustration against his pillow, but he wasn't all that successful.

'I'll find us something low cost, and not travel too far. That way we can have more than one honeymoon.' Sherlock sounded almost reasonable as he said this, but then his tone changed and John found it hard not to strangle him. 'Besides, I might have to return at a moment's notice. I can't go too far from the work after all. Scotland Yard would never survive the shock.'

Choosing not to respond to this shining example of his husband's conceit John closed his eyes tightly.

Sleep, which had been so close to his fingertips only minutes earlier, took some time to reach him. But when it finally came, rest didn't come with it.

CHAPTER NINE

Two Years Ago – Afghanistan

'STAY WITH ME. COME ON! NO, DON'T YOU BLOODY DARE, PRIVATE, THAT'S AN ORDER!'

The road on which the ambulance travelled was the usual dusty unremarkable track through what had once been dusty unremarkable farmland before greed and political upheaval turned it into a warzone.

John didn't have the mental bandwidth to pay attention to the view, not with an injured soldier under his hands who would certainly lose his arm, if they ever stabilised him enough not to lose his life. But, as hard as he was concentrating, some deep-seated survival instinct still made John look towards the front passenger window, and the growing speck approaching just above the ground.

There was a girl standing by the side of the road, waving her arms in a desperate sort of signal. He knew her. Of the few locals that he'd spoken to often, hers was the face he wouldn't forget. She'd looked so grateful when he saved her sister, even though he couldn't save her.

A dead girl wanted his attention.

John's brain finally realised what was heading toward the ambulance.

He shouted, not specific words, not that he could remember, but he knew he shouted as he folded himself protectively over his patient's body. The shout hadn't helped. By the time he'd seen it there was nothing in the laws of physics that could have prevented the RPG from making contact with the convoy.

There was a moment of weightlessness as the vehicle rolled, medical equipment mixed with things he never wanted to think about hanging suspended in the air, before gravity reasserted itself again.

The rear compartment of the ambulance shattered as it hit the ground, splitting along one side and spewing its contents across the compacted dirt. Later John would realise the collapse had prevented the vehicle continuing its tumble and had saved him from being crushed by either the patient's trolley or the chassis of the ambulance itself. At the time all he saw was the blood and the waste.

Tomlinson was dead. At least she'd died instantly. Brennon wasn't so lucky. He was looking back at John from the driver's seat, a mess of shrapnel and open wounds.

John tried to stand. He tried to scramble through the mess of fire and broken vehicle to reach his colleague, to do his fucking job, to save a man's life. He tried. But he couldn't.

His left foot wouldn't respond to his instructions. Instead it stretched heavy and useless behind him. John knew that if he thought about it he'd feel the pain of the compound fracture, the shrapnel, the sticky heat of blood. But now was not the time for thinking.

He tried to pull himself forward on his arms but he felt too dizzy and weak to manage. A concussion perhaps? He dismissed the thought. It didn't matter why he was failing to do his duty, only that he was.

Brennon was watching him, blood seeping from his mouth.

There wasn't anything John could do but hold his gaze. Witnessing his passing was the very least he could do.

The insurgents would appear soon, their battered old Jeep dragging a dust cloud behind it, and the shooting would begin. But for now there was just Brennon's ragged breathing and the wet noise of the ruptured diesel tank giving up its fuel across the sand.

Dreaming, John watched, waiting for the light to go out of those pained eyes, just like they did every night, just like they had for three fucking months of nightmares. But Brennon didn't blink. He just kept on staring into John's soul.

Any second now he'd hear Private Malik's faint cries from where he lay under the ruined stretcher inches to his left. Then he could move, then he could help someone he could reach.

Brennon didn't blink. Time didn't move. There was just that awful wet breathing and life's blood seeping across the dirt.

He could hear the thumping of his own heart against his eardrums.

His leg hurt. It hurt so fucking much and he had to ignore it, he had to witness this, he had to...

Two Years Ago – Marylebone, London

'John?' The voice was distant and unreal. 'John, I'm coming in!'

He couldn't focus on it. Brennon's eyes filled his mind.

'Jesus, what a mess.' There was that voice again. Closer. Concerned, but irritated, too. 'Come on, man, wake up! I can't lift you off the floor!'

A hand closed around his ankle, tugging backwards.

John woke with a shriek.

Someone groaned and let go of him.

Having woken so abruptly from one of his recurring nightmares John knew it would be a moment or two before reality properly reasserted itself. So while his brain came back online John took the opportunity to look around without much of the context that would normally cloud his opinions.

The room was bland in a 'builder's grade magnolia-coloured paint and discount carpet' kind of way. Certainly, much easier on the eye than the rather lumberjack-esque decor in the flat he'd been renting from a friend. Sometimes plain and boring was better than weird but interesting.

Beside him the 'someone' groaned again.

His brain reminded him of the existence of Sherlock Holmes whilst immediately erasing that last thought. Weird but interesting and very, very good looking was infinitely preferable to, well, anything else.

How on earth had John managed to forget the man he'd accidentally ended up flat sharing with for the last month?

The figure behind him gave a louder, angrier groan.

He glanced sideways and realised Sherlock was also on the floor, clutching at his crotch.

'Fucking hell, John!'

John felt a little guilty – he hadn't meant to kick out after all, but he'd had to shake off the source of pain. It wasn't as if he'd intended to catch the other man square in the bollocks.

Still, there was no reason for Sherlock to be dragging him out of bed! His thoughts stilled, listening for any alarms or sirens that might actually constitute an emergency. Nope. Everything was silent.

'Why are you in my room?' he asked, choosing to go for indignation over apology.

'There was a thud and then you were screaming!' Sherlock hissed as he clambered up from the floor and collapsed heavily onto the bed, his hands still cradling his aching privates. 'I might be able to ignore that – not that I'd want to – but Mrs Hudson has had more than enough noise complaints over the years. I would much rather she not peg me for a sadist on top of everything else.'

John stared up at him. Sherlock's movements drew his attention to his own awkward position sprawled half on the floor with his legs still on the bed. No wonder his leg hurt so much.

'Noise complaints, huh?' he asked. 'Loud boyfriends?'

'Oh, no, that's all me...' Sherlock said with a grin that faded to a look that could almost be mistaken for introspection. 'And I might have shot the wall a bit. Caused a few explosions. Blown out four windows. Got into a fist fight with three cockneys and a macaque. Fell down the stairs.'

John could feel his sleep-addled brain doing somersaults in its effort to keep up with all these revelations. One thing seemed to lodge in the gears so he couldn't process anything else. 'Wait, a macaque like...a monkey? You fought a monkey?'

The effort at looking shamefaced was probably Sherlock's best, but it was still pretty terrible. Whatever had happened Sherlock was pretty proud of it.

'It's a long story,' Sherlock said, glancing at the bedside table. 'And it's 4am.'

John followed his eye line and remembered again that he was lying on the floor.

'Shit!' John gasped. 'Sorry.'

He hauled himself upright on stiff limbs that seemed determined to embarrass him, but Sherlock didn't seem to notice his stumbling.

Once Sherlock even started to reach out to steady him but he seemed to realise John's pride wouldn't appreciate it and lowered his hand.

John gave him a grateful smile and flopped down next to him.

'It's okay, I wasn't asleep.'

'You're wearing your dressing gown,' John said, taking in the skinny shins and bare, bony feet protruding from the bottom of the item in question. He tried not to be obvious about letting his gaze drift upward but the exposed strip of sparse chest hair gave him pause.

'And?' Sherlock said with an amused twist to his lips.

John didn't have an answer to that, so he just raised an eyebrow and tried to play cool.

Despite living in Sherlock's home for over a month John hadn't learned all that much about him yet.

What had started out as a mysterious interlude had become a permanent arrangement, thanks to John's friend suddenly deciding to rent his flat, but since 221b Baker Street was more convenient for every part of John's mostly empty life, he hadn't hesitated long before he asked Sherlock to let him officially move in. Sherlock had seemed surprised by the question; not because John wanted to stay, but because he seemed to think they'd already agreed that he would.

Though when they could have agreed to such a thing John really didn't know. Sherlock had vanished for the first three weeks after John arrived. Every day since then had been either a flurry of activity as he bounced from case to case, while the rare moments when Sherlock had no work to occupy him were spent in mostly comfortable silence as they both pursued their own occupations.

They were housemates, nothing more.

Well, until right this second.

Perhaps it was just the effect of waking up from such a horrible dream but something had changed. John couldn't entirely put his finger on it.

The part of his brain governing 'good manners' clearly hadn't come online yet. John stared intently at Sherlock while he tried to work out what was different about the man.

No, odd choice of clothing aside, he couldn't find anything out of place about that attractive but difficult to read face.

At least Sherlock didn't seem to be in pain any more. John really hadn't meant to kick him. Certainly not *there*, anyway.

Sherlock blinked a few times, apparently uncomfortable with receiving the kind of scrutiny he usually doled out, and letting his own gaze drift away, his expression sobered as he changed the subject. 'Flashbacks?'

'Of a sort,' John said, also looking away to pick at a loose thread at the edge of the cheap duvet cover. He really didn't want to talk about the way his flashbacks turned into paralysing nightmares. Reliving the incident over and over was bad enough without becoming trapped in it.

Instead of the questions he was expecting to be asked, John found a cool hand resting gently over his own. He met Sherlock's eye just in time to see him hide away his nervous expression. As he stared at the man's blushing profile he suddenly realised why this felt different. Sherlock had never actually set foot in this room, and, now he thought about it, the man hadn't ever got near enough to touch unless it was absolutely necessary.

In fact, John hadn't seen Sherlock this close up since–

He swallowed and couldn't stop his eyes from dropping to Sherlock's lips. He hadn't been this close to Sherlock since he'd kissed him in that cafe.

'You know,' Sherlock began, rousing John from that very pleasant memory. He coughed and began to flush an even deeper shade of red. 'I, uh, have a little experience with nightmares and flashbacks myself, and I heard that distraction can help…'

John felt his eyebrow rising again without any conscious input from his brain. 'Can it now?'

'Mm-hmm.' Sherlock's gaze was wandering now but his hand hadn't moved. 'For example, if you were always following the same bedtime routine, then a change might help—'

'Like what?' John had his suspicions but Sherlock couldn't mean—

'Well…' The beautiful man beside him said quietly, 'like not sleeping alone?'

John wanted to pinch himself but he couldn't think of a subtle way to do it. He had to be dreaming. This sort of thing did not happen to him.

Somehow, without consulting him at all, his mouth said, 'Sounds like you're coming on to me.'

'Not when you've just woken screaming and traumatised, no,' Sherlock said stiffly, with no small amount of offence in his voice.

John turned his hand to squeeze those thin musician's fingers. 'Sherlock, I didn't know you cared.'

'Then you're even less observant than I originally suspected,' Sherlock said. He was looking away but John could see the blush still burning in his ears.

'But would you?' John asked. If this was a dream then John had nothing to lose and if this were real, well, he could probably blame it all on lack of sleep if Sherlock was offended. Somehow John didn't really think he would be.

'Would I what?' Sherlock responded, with a frown.

'Would you come on to me?' he elaborated, with a huff. 'If I hadn't just woken up screaming? During the day, when I have all my wits about me?'

The look Sherlock gave him was made of equal parts incredulity and frustration. 'I rather thought I had been!'

'When?'

'Lots of times.'

John rolled his eyes but couldn't help smiling at the exaggerated look of disappointment on Sherlock's face. 'I'm not that oblivious, am I?'

'Yes.'

'You didn't need to agree quite so emphatically,' John laughed, then cut himself off with a yawn. He would have expected Sherlock's admission of interest to make his heart race but instead it settled over him like a warm blanket. The knowledge that Sherlock actually *like* liked him made him feel safe in a way he couldn't really describe. After stifling another yawn he continued, 'But you can explain my stupidity in the morning. Do you really want to stay? Because you're right, it might help.'

Sherlock squeezed his hand. Instead of answering he just leant forward.

The kiss was a soft, chaste thing, not on the lips but at the corner, where John's overnight stubble didn't quite reach so the skin was still smooth and delicate.

He couldn't have asked for a more perfect start.

John turned just enough to capture Sherlock's lips with his own in a closed mouth kiss that echoed the sweetness of the first. He didn't try for more but instead he let Sherlock guide him down onto the mattress.

The bed was a twin, narrow and barely enough for his own anxious, nightmare-wracked body at times, but somehow with Sherlock curled up behind him it was just the right size.

They shared an odd first night together.

For one, John was certain that Sherlock didn't sleep at all that night. He laid quietly with his chest pressed tight to John's back, one arm slung over John's waist, breathing evenly, but John could swear he could hear his brain whirring in the dark.

Despite that, or possibly because of it, John had his first sound sleep in what felt like forever. Even before the desert attack – before he'd even taken his commission as a medical officer, in fact – John had not slept well. Somehow he felt safe knowing that

Sherlock was there behind him, his mind working on a hundred different problems but his body still present for John's sake.

Whatever attempts at flirtation John had missed he found he didn't really care.

He fell asleep knowing that tomorrow he was going to do his damnedest not to let this chance go to waste; no matter how strange dating a consulting detective might be.

CHAPTER TEN

Present Day – York

UNSURPRISINGLY, THE RAILWAY MUSEUM *DID* CONTAIN TRAINS. A GREAT many trains. Quite frankly far more trains than John had ever expected or wanted to see in his lifetime.

He couldn't really complain, though. Well, technically he could, but he wouldn't. He knew Sherlock and his habits – complaining never helped. So on those grounds he chose not to gripe about this latest excursion.

Besides, perhaps Sherlock *was* intending to surprise him with some grand romantic gesture.

John snorted to himself in amusement at the idea and earned himself an elbow in the ribs.

'What's funny?' Sherlock asked while he peered up at some huge old steam engine like he actually cared about the neat informative sign stuck to one of the wheels.

'Everything,' John said. The exercise of crossing the city had helped to improve his mood this time. The sun had been shining brightly and they'd followed a long, circuitous route that avoided most of the tourist traps. Perhaps that was the secret to John's low mood – he needed to get away from people for a while. Somewhere warm and close to nature.

He shook his head with a smile and let his eyes drift around the big concrete space filled with tourists and machinery.

There was a man standing in the train cab to their left, wearing an authentic period costume and a bemused expression as he poked at the dials. Suddenly he seemed to become aware of John's gaze and turned, briefly revealing marks that could have been burns on the back of his waistcoat before he moved out of view.

Probably just a reenactor. Nothing to worry about. Even if there was no obvious way to access the train car from the ground.

Trying to forget everything else, John did his best to look around again with Gloria's case in the forefront of his mind.

It didn't help.

If there was any clue to the reason for them being at this particular museum he couldn't see it. But then, he rarely could. That was Sherlock's job, and Sherlock wasn't letting anything slip.

The man in question frowned, but didn't look at him. 'Everything?'

'We're supposed to be on our honeymoon, but you've brought me to an educational museum,' John grumbled, 'when we both know that you don't much care to learn anything unless it's relevant to a case.'

Okay, perhaps he was going to complain about this after all. The floor beneath his feet was cold, hard concrete and no matter how good his boots were, the chill was beginning to seep into his bones. The ache in his leg was becoming impossible to ignore.

'Maybe it *is* for a case.'

John sighed and pinched his nose. Of course, he knew this was for a case. Gloria's case. He should have just said something on the train, but he hadn't and now getting Sherlock to tell him the truth of his own free will felt like the most important thing in the world.

'If there really is a case involving a train that—' John looked up at the sign Sherlock was still pretending to read, 'hasn't moved under its own power since 1934, then I'd say it's a little past the point where we could be any help.'

Sherlock finally looked at him. He didn't turn his head but his eyes slid slowly across to meet John's gaze.

They stared at one another for a silent beat, something clearly curling at the edge of Sherlock's consciousness and waiting to be said.

Suddenly John wasn't sure he wanted to know why Sherlock had chosen to lie to him. What if it was awful? What if it tore apart what equilibrium they had? The nature of Sherlock's work was such that they never really experienced true contentment, but did John want to risk it all just to…

A tourist with a camera as large as her head barged between them. The tension broke.

'Come on!' Sherlock said to him with a grin. John's hand was grasped in his before John had consciously realised that it was being offered and they were off.

Weaving through the crowds of tourists inside the museum felt no different to being in London, though the streets of London rarely contained quite so many trains.

John laughed, once more amused by his own ridiculous thoughts and pleased by the smile that was finally gracing Sherlock's face again. He'd been so quiet on the walk across the city that John would almost have thought he was angry at him, if it weren't for the way he kept his arm around John's waist for most of the journey.

That felt nice. It was the sort of public display that Sherlock only indulged in occasionally, and John was determined to make the most of it.

After weaving their way between the engines in the main hall Sherlock pulled John into a slightly smaller room that was absolutely crammed with towering glass cabinets. There were narrow aisles between each row but even these seemed to be losing the battle against the encroaching mass of, well, stuff.

There wasn't really a better word for it all. 'Artifacts' sounded ancient, 'specimens' made him chuckle, and 'objects' just didn't capture the sheer randomness of what he was seeing. Everything seemed to be train and railway-related, but some of it must have had the most tenuous of links.

In a way, the room reminded John of university libraries, or perhaps the storage department at the Victoria & Albert museum that Sherlock always managed to get lost in. Places that the public weren't really supposed to see, where visual elegance was sacrificed for the sake of maximising the storage space.

John was just beginning to look around properly, half concerned they'd wandered into a restricted area, when Sherlock drew him close against his side and pressed an unexpected kiss to his lips. All of John's worries flittered out of his head. They would come back to roost sooner or later, but for now he resolved to enjoy the sensation of Sherlock's body heat through their shirts.

It soon became clear that this oddly-crowded space was open to the public, though most of the visitors were cutting through the room to something on the other side.

Sherlock, however, seemed to be determined to look at every single item on display.

Again John glanced around, this time with a slight but rising worry.

There must be thousands of objects crammed into this room.

They'd be stuck here for hours.

But time moved more comfortably with Sherlock's arm around his waist. Within five minutes John wasn't even looking into the cabinets any more. He had his face resting against Sherlock's chest, almost dozing as they moved slowly down each aisle in turn. Here amongst the shelves it was mostly quiet enough that he could focus on just the sound of Sherlock's breathing.

Calm.

Peaceful.

Relaxing.

Exactly what a holiday *should* be.

John reluctantly opened his eyes when Sherlock made an odd noise of satisfaction.

By the entrance the display cases had contained items from the earliest days of commercial train travel. The shelves behind Sherlock now were just as dusty, but they were filled with the faded neon colours of a more recent era.

A date caught John's eye on the crumpled edge of an old timetable – 1982.

But Sherlock hadn't been looking at that, he'd been looking at something over John's shoulder.

John turned to find a wall so completely covered in framed images that there was barely a square inch of brick left visible between them.

Some of the frames actually touched the concrete floors while others were lost far overhead amongst the rafters.

Although he could have just asked what had interested Sherlock, John preferred to work it out for himself. Sherlock would laugh at him whatever he did, but he felt better when he at least tried to keep up.

All the photographs were in black and white, scenes of local everyday life that usually appeared in dull regional newspapers.

A picture just below eye level showed a crowded railway platform just like any other on a busy summer day. Crowds dressed in a mix of power suits and bright sundresses. Almost everyone had a perm and the same tired expression – John didn't remember much of the decade himself but he knew that times had been hard.

No one wonder everyone looked stressed.

Well, almost everyone.

One figure stood out from the crowd, but there was no sane reason for Sherlock to have come here looking for her in old press photographs. There must have been thousands of pictures taken in the busy streets of York that year, but how often would a photographer have got the names from an entire crowd? And yet Sherlock had found her. He'd found Gloria.

She'd been a little difficult to recognise at first glance, her face sunken by pain or medication, and her hair wrapped in a patterned scarf, but standing by the luggage lockers with a key in her hand Gloria had looked up at the photographer and flashed the camera the brightest smile she could.

'Come on.' Sherlock slipped his arm through John's to gently lead him away.

John didn't bother to resist.

Sherlock wasn't saying anything about the photograph. Just like he hadn't said anything about the books at that medieval hall or the real reason they were here 'on holiday.'

The original case hadn't seemed important enough to warrant this kind of secrecy – a missing woman who was long since dead and an indeterminate inheritance. What about that was worth sneaking around over?

John had tolerated Sherlock's strange behaviour so far. Well, he'd tolerated a certain amount of weirdness the entire time they'd known one another. But a line had to be drawn somewhere.

John had known more or less exactly what Sherlock was going to ask before they'd even reached the information desk in the main hall.

'Hello, I'm here about the left luggage,' The detective began in his most charming yet officious tone.

Apparently, the middle-aged man wearing a 'volunteer' badge was immune to Sherlock's charms. He didn't bother to look up as he pointed left. 'The lockers are in the corridor between the exhibition halls.'

'Not–' Sherlock tried to start again but there was no chance of getting a word in edgeways.

'That way.'

'I–' Sherlock didn't even manage to get a syllable out this time.

'Over there,' the volunteer repeated, as if he was speaking to a small child who didn't understand directions yet.

John had to cover his mouth to stifle a laugh at Sherlock's baffled expression. They were used to being dismissed – private detectives were the stuff of fiction to most people – but they mostly managed to ask at least the first question before they were sent on their way.

Someone behind them sighed heavily. 'Can I help you gentlemen? Since Gareth here is apparently incapable of helping anyone.'

'Luggage lockers are that way,' Gareth the volunteer repeated once more before turning his back on them all.

The newcomer was a stately looking woman with neat grey hair and an air of being tired of idiots. The look on her face expressed a hope that the two of them weren't just new idiots for her to deal with.

'I'm looking for Marilyn?' Sherlock began, 'We recently spoke over email about an item of left luggage that I believe is in one of your displays? She was going to find it for us.'

'I am Marilyn,' she said, extending a hand that promised a handshake firm enough to make John's knuckles ache with preemptive pain.

'Sherlock. This is John.' Only John would notice the wince in Sherlock's voice as he released her hand, or the way he subtly flexed his fingers while he continued speaking.

'As I said in my email, I'm looking for some *historical* information about some left luggage,' Sherlock said, emphasising the word historical in the direction of the unhelpful volunteer. The man didn't seem to notice. 'A bag that was left at the station in the early '80s. According to your online archives it was moved here.'

Her only reply for a moment or two was a low 'hmmm,' but she waved them towards a row of benches that seemed to have been placed specifically to take advantage of the sun streaming through the tall, dusty windows. John waited for Marilyn to seat herself before dropping onto the other end of the bench with a suppressed noise of satisfaction that was mostly covered by Sherlock settling himself between them.

'If you're looking for secret Cold War messages I'm afraid you're out of luck,' she said with a kind smile. 'Firstly because almost everything from that era of the station's history is long gone, and secondly because I don't think spies ever actually used anything so obvious.'

John blinked. 'Why would we be looking for Cold War secrets?' he asked, even as he realised that such a thing would be a good explanation for Sherlock's odd behaviour.

A glance at Sherlock's face suggested otherwise, though – he looked as confused as John felt.

'Our investigation isn't anything to do with espionage, I…damn.' Sherlock stopped and looked guiltily at John for a moment before he tried to start over.

Marilyn cut him off before he got out another word.

'This isn't some kind of illuminati nonsense, either, is it?' she asked, with more than a hint of distaste. 'Because we have enough of that as it is!'

'What?' John had lost track of this conversation almost immediately but now he was completely at sea.

'No,' Sherlock said reassuringly, 'no, it's just a classic family scandal or two. Gossip column stuff, not the kind of thing to bring down a government any more.'

The 'any more' seemed significant, though John didn't feel confident enough in what was going on to actually know for sure. He tried to make his brain pay more attention.

Marilyn nodded, apparently satisfied that they weren't going to drag her into whatever it was that she disapproved of so much.

'Okay, then,' she said, 'Well, I did some research for you, but as I mentioned the lockers from that era are long gone. These days most luggage storage is for a set period of time and you have to leave your details for security reasons. Back then it was all coin-operated. You put the coin in the slot, closed the door, turned the key, and everything was secure until you came back with the key. It wasn't very efficient. People lost keys and decided the items weren't worth coming back for, or they forgot that they'd left anything behind at all. By the time they were torn out in the early '90s I think maybe ten percent of the lockers had something long-forgotten left in them. We advertised briefly in the local papers, then more or less everything was auctioned off or destroyed.'

'Except the item you're looking for.'

This felt like an unnecessarily long way of saying 'yes, we have what you're looking for' but Marilyn seemed to be the kind of person who enjoyed the sound of her own voice. John had had a lot of experience being married to just such a person so he chose not to comment out loud.

'You found it, then?' Sherlock sounded a little surprised, like he'd expected to be told the item was lost or untraceable.

John wondered why they'd come all this way without checking, but this hadn't been their first stop so maybe whatever Sherlock was looking for wasn't all that vital to the case.

'It took us a while,' Marilyn confirmed, with a nod of pride. 'It wasn't actually in the main collection as such. Have you seen our period displays? Some of the trains have been restored, or partially restored, to show daily life in their original era. There's a medical carriage, fully furnished royal carriages, et cetera. If we can source them we prefer to use original artifacts.'

'Are you saying that the '80s were long enough ago to be recreated in a museum?' John asked, with a laugh that he immediately quelled. 'It is, isn't it? Bloody hell, I feel old now.'

'Imagine how I feel,' Marilyn replied. She managed to stay deadpan just long enough that John felt extra guilty about the joke before she finally laughed herself. 'But yes, we have a carriage from that era with original posters and timetables displayed on it; some of the tables set up with an early mobile phone and a, uh, 'boombox' I think it was called; that kind of thing. Your 'Miss Gloria Evans' left us an entire bag full of personal items, I think that's why it was saved, it's very evocative of the era. You're welcome to look, provided you don't touch anything without asking first, of course.'

'Of course,' Sherlock repeated. He wore the happy smile of someone who never asked permission, but also rarely got caught.

As Marilyn led them on a winding path through the exhibits John followed with the skeptical look of a man who both thought his time was being wasted, but very much feared it wasn't.

CHAPTER ELEVEN

Present Day – York

THEY SAT ON A BENCH BY THE RIVER, DUCKS NIBBLING AT THE GRASS AT their feet and a notebook in a transparent plastic bag filling the too-wide space between them.

The sun was hot out here away from the concrete and steel of the museum, but the heat radiating up from the bench wasn't enough to take the chill off John's bones. Judging by Sherlock's paler-than-usual skin and the slight tremble in his jaw, Sherlock was feeling much the same.

John didn't think he'd ever actually expected to find the bag.

The restored train carriage had smelled more of cleaning products than John had been expecting based on the memories of his youth. It seemed that the exhibit had been very well scrubbed before it went on display and only dust had been stirred up since then.

That artificial-lemon scent kept drifting through his senses even now, sitting out here in a little isolated section of parkland between a bridge and a jetty advertising boat tours of the city. Perhaps the smell had soaked into their clothes, or into the documents currently separating them like the bulk of a mountain.

Even with permission from the museum John had still felt a little strange standing at one end of the carriage separated from the public by a sheet of Plexiglas. It had made him feel oddly dissonant with reality that everything on display around him was probably the same age as him. He hadn't said anything at the time. Sherlock treated everything like it was an exhibit to be studied, and Marilyn had already expressed her own discomfort at the idea. There had been no point in irritating someone who was helping them.

One of the large tables inside the train carriage had been set up to look like it had just been abandoned by a group of untidy commuters.

Newspapers had been strewn across most of its surface – a sight that was oddly reminiscent of their own journey to the city – but sitting there in the middle of it all was a notepad open to a page filled with familiar handwriting.

'Now, what are the odds of that?' he'd asked Sherlock in a tone of both surprise and deep suspicion.

The reply he got was one he'd never seen from Sherlock before – a look of mute shock that lasted for only a heartbeat before the detective had recovered to look not at the book, but at a navy and neon pink bag that had been artfully arranged on one of the seats.

There had been, in the end, little of interest in the bag. A few magazines about celebrities John had never heard of; make-up; several scarves; a change of clothes; a yellowed map of the city; crumpled receipts and the other detritus of daily life. A life that had been lived by someone who knew they were dying.

While Marilyn and Sherlock had been focused on emptying the bag, item by item, John had heard a tourist at the open end of the carriage ask whether this was some kind of entertainment. He'd turned away from that unwelcome intrusion from the real world and found himself staring down at the notebook instead. At Gloria's diary.

The book had been left open on a page filled with notes about the Minster that stood in the centre of the city. Although her handwriting seemed to have deteriorated a little further, the sketches filling the margins were drawn with a neat and careful hand. The page had been undated but there was no mention of the fire that had badly damaged the building in 1984.

He had reached out, intending to turn the page and look for a date, then remembered himself and peered at the edges of the pages instead. Only three or four more after this one showed any sign of being dog-eared, and the back half of the book looked to be entirely untouched.

Marilyn had taken the book then, slipping it into a sturdy plastic bag after Sherlock promised her he'd take good care of it.

So here it was, sitting on the bench between them, the last diary.

'I don't think she lived for very long after she left London,' John said, back in the present. He wished the smell of bleach would leave his nostrils. The scent made him think of hospices and inevitability.

Sherlock turned his head to look at him but said nothing.

For his own part John kept on staring out at the water. He let the silence own its awkwardness.

Out of nowhere a wind whipped around them, rustling the leaves in the trees and making both men shiver.

It was gone almost as soon as it appeared, but the breeze seemed to have shaken something loose in Sherlock's throat.

'I'm sorry.'

Sherlock didn't say for what, but the words were so heartfelt that John was almost tempted to forgive him before he'd even received an explanation.

Almost.

'Two years.' John said. 'However you count it – from the thief in Tottenham Court station or that poor lad in New Malden – I've been working cases with you for two years. Over and over I've ended up working without you ever actually asking me if I want to be involved. I can't–' John stopped and pursed his lips, unsure of where he really wanted this to go next.

'I can't keep on not knowing. Involve me or don't. Let me do my job or have me work with you, but don't keep tricking me like this.'

John let his eyes follow the flow of the river out of the city centre, away from Sherlock.

He couldn't keep letting this happen, even if it had been the way things started.

Two Years Ago – New Malden, London

Of course, John understood, in an academic sense, that Sherlock

111

was a 'detective'. John had even been accidentally involved in two of the man's cases back when they'd first met, though he still didn't know what exactly had gone on with either of them.

That, really, was the problem—he understood Sherlock's job title, but not the job itself. Or rather, how 'detection' was actually achieved.

In the six weeks since they'd first shared a bed, Sherlock was either absent from the flat, or pottering around in a way that seemed calculated to drive John to distraction. He almost wanted to help but he hadn't the faintest idea of where to start. He couldn't end every case by tripping people up, it had been a fluke that it worked the first two times. John would have to somehow turn into Sherlock's live-in assistant. A medically trained side-kick, if you will.

John snorted at the thought of the pair of them in Lycra superhero outfits. The whole idea was ludicrous.

Besides, he had his own job to look for now that his leg was almost healed. Not that he wanted to think about that right now.

'How does it work?' John asked quietly after the waitress dropped off their drinks at the table. 'Your job, I mean.'

They were sitting in one of the many Korean restaurants in New Malden, an area of London south of the river that John had never visited before but Sherlock seemed to know like the back of his hand.

He could almost have believed it was a date. John wasn't sure about that, no matter how much he wanted it to be a date. Sherlock hadn't actually asked him out as such, rather he'd just asked if John was busy and when John said 'no' he'd been led out of the flat with barely a long enough pause to put his shoes on.

The journey was little more than ten miles, but with trains that were slow and hellishly overcrowded it took them well over an hour to reach their destination. Normally John might have been irritated by that, or by the fact that they'd been forced to stand for the entire journey, but he'd rather enjoyed being pressed against Sherlock's chest all that time.

Now that they were sitting, John's leg was beginning to register its complaints. He'd only recently progressed to using a single cane and the limb wasn't used to this kind of treatment. He ignored it in favour of watching the way Sherlock's lips cradled the glass as he took a sip of maesil-ju.

'People ask me to investigate things, I investigate them,' Sherlock said with a shrug.

John really had been hoping for a more detailed answer than that. He took a sip from his own glass, absently noting the unexpected sweetness of the plum wine as he tried to formulate a question that couldn't be brushed off so easily.

At last he settled on, 'But why not ask the police?'

That, at least, seemed to hold Sherlock's attention a little better.

'Things aren't always a matter for the police,' he said, leaning forward a little so he could rest his elbow on the table and swirl the wine in his glass as he spoke.

'Do you know how much crime goes unrecorded in this country? Especially in London. Ten to twenty percent. A minor theft; a suspected break-in where nothing seems to be taken; a dispute between neighbours; a fight with no serious injuries. Or maybe there's no crime at all. Perhaps someone suspects another person or business of shady dealings that might, if proven, result in a successful action in a civil court but they don't know how to prove that.'

As he spoke the fingers on Sherlock's free hand were flexing as if in time with something, some kind of music that John couldn't hear, but wished he could.

'Or someone is concerned about a person who might be missing, but they're not close enough for them to be sure,' he continued, then pointed at John like he'd just remembered something. 'You know, one of the most interesting cases I ever dealt with was brought to me by a little old lady who was convinced a local dog walker had been replaced by a 'pod person'. They looked the same but they suddenly followed a slightly different routine for odd periods of time – crossing the road in a different place for three days, that kind of thing. Can you imagine what the police would say to that?'

'They would have referred her to a mental health team,' John said. He found himself leaning forward too, mirroring Sherlock's pose. 'Were they twins?'

Sherlock snorted. 'That would *not* be an interesting case!'

Trying to be offended by Sherlock's tone John countered, 'Okay then, what did make it interesting?'

Here Sherlock leaned forward over the narrow table even more, ostensibly for the sake of privacy, but John almost suspected that he enjoyed the way John shivered as his breath brushed the back of his hand.

'Well,' he said with a smile, 'I had no other cases and nothing better to do, so I decided to stakeout this mysterious, allegedly alien dog walker, and you know what I found out about them in a month of watching the street?'

Again John followed Sherlock's change in position. They were close enough to kiss, which was possibly the point, but the melodramatic storytelling was holding John captivated.

'What?' he asked.

'Absolutely nothing of interest!' Sherlock laughed. 'Nothing at all! The world's most boring androgynous person in the world, you could have set the atomic clock by their routine, hell, you could have set it by the dog, too.'

'But, isn't that interesting in itself?' John frowned as he tried to follow the thread that had suddenly got away from him. 'Surely normal people don't work like that.'

Sherlock waved a hand dismissively and took another sip of his wine.

'I've never met a 'normal' person so I wouldn't know. Normal is just the average of a vast population,' he said. 'But no, it's not that uncommon. People get into routines. Have you ever seen a cleared house that was once occupied by the same person for decades? You can often trace the path of their daily routine by the wear on the fixtures and floor coverings. You've only been in our flat for two months and I already know that you always wake just after six whether you get up or not; you always avoid that one squeaky floorboard on the way down the stairs but going back up your leg won't let you step over it; and you only ever mastur–'

The word was cut off by John slapping a hand over Sherlock's mouth.

He felt Sherlock's face shift into a grin against his skin for an instant just before Sherlock licked his palm.

'Fine, I get the point!' John said irritably as he wiped his hand on his jeans. He could feel the blush of humiliation racing over his skin but he did his best to pretend it wasn't happening. 'So, there was no case? The woman really should have been referred to her GP?'

'Oh, yes, that would have made things a lot easier, though they'd still have needed me to catch the culprits.'

Just as John was going to utter a slightly outraged and baffled 'what?' the conversation was interrupted by the arrival of the waitress. John was amused to see that they'd both ordered short ribs, served mild in broth for him, sweet with rice for Sherlock. The next few minutes were taken up by chewing and appreciative noises but Sherlock finally carried on where he'd left off.

'You see,' he said, 'if she'd been sent to her GP she might have been tested for the usual culprits for mild disorientation – fever, early signs of dementia, malnutrition–'

'Drugs and alcohol,' John supplied, finally seeing where this was going.

'Exactly!' Sherlock cried a little louder than John would have liked if he hadn't been so engrossed in the story. 'Exactly! The qualified doctor sees it at last! While I'd taken the case and had spent a lot of time in the area, I don't usually eat when I'm working–'

'You didn't eat for a month!' If John sounded horrified and incredulous that's because he was both and he didn't really care if Sherlock noticed.

'Ha, no, of course not, but I do try to limit my consumption – and I never eat while I'm actively on the job – which is why I wasn't affected by the hallucinogenic that was being introduced to the water supply. You see, the woman who came to me lived in a cul-de-sac, a little isolated spur of about fifteen houses all receiving water through the same pipelines. The whole thing was a cover-up for the slow burglary of an estate that backed onto my client's property. It was only when I spoke to her and she reported entirely different events to the ones I'd seen myself that I realised there was something odd going on.'

John frowned at him, his spoon only halfway to his mouth. 'That seems rather melodramatic for a robbery, doesn't it?'

'Depends what you're stealing, and how badly you don't want to get caught,' Sherlock laughed. 'And what sort of scrabble tile name the organisation that'll come looking for you might have.'

'Hmmm.' The John of just a few months ago wouldn't have believed him much, but the still-recent memories of being observed by nameless men in suits gave just enough credence to the story for it to ring true to the John sitting right here.

'Most of my cases aren't that bizarre,' Sherlock said quietly towards his plate, like he knew John was still skeptical and wasn't willing to look at a doubtful expression.

He'd finally put his glass down, his fingers resting on the table just close enough to John's own that he could feel the warmth from his skin.

'You know, one of the easiest cases I've had recently ended in a very strange way. I'm not sure most people would believe it. I infiltrated a gang passing stolen jewellery though a network of agents hiding in plain sight, and – would you believe it – some handsome army doctor trips the head of the local branch with his crutches.'

John tried to hold back his flattered smile as he replied, 'That is strange – you knowing two army doctors with crutches.'

He moved his hand just enough to rest against Sherlock's and was pleased enough to grin when Sherlock shifted his hand to weave their fingers together.

'Mmm, well, I don't know any with crutches any more, just a walking stick,' Sherlock said, glancing up with a smirk. 'And definitely much better looking, now the regulation haircut is growing out.'

The compliment made John blush but he didn't argue. Over the last few weeks he'd found Sherlock usually backed up his compliments with evidence that rather spoiled the romantic mood.

'So, was that the incident in the Tube?' John asked. 'Or the one at St James's?'

Sherlock looked up at him with a hint of surprise in his eyes, but he recovered quickly. 'The Tube. It's a long story I mostly can't share with you in public just yet. The other...' He shrugged and went back to his meal.

For his part John tried to do the same, but even as he enjoyed the excellent food in front of him he had to wonder at just how little Sherlock could share with him, even though he'd been there himself.

Was this how a relationship with Sherlock was always going to be?

The thought almost made him choke on a mouthful of radish.

Was that even what this was? A relationship? They hadn't even slept together yet – well, no, they'd literally *slept* together plenty in the weeks since Sherlock had woken him from that first bad nightmare – but Sherlock seemed very willing to take his time with the physical aspects of this relationship, if it even was a relationship.

'Oh, god,' John muttered, dropping his head into his hand while his mind spiralled into a ridiculous line of questions he really couldn't formulate to make any kind of sense.

Sherlock looked up in concern and John could feel his face flushing with embarrassment.

Just as he opened his mouth, apparently to ask John if he was okay, their meal was again interrupted by a member of the restaurant staff. This time, however, he was carrying a manila folder full of paper instead of more food.

'I'm sorry to interrupt you, Mr Holmes,' the man began. 'But you did say you'd have a look at my son's case.'

The restaurant owner – because that's who the man turned out to be – was at least apologetic for interrupting their date with business. But since the man had also agreed with Sherlock in advance that the meal was on the house John didn't feel like he was the one who should be apologising in the first place.

Not that Sherlock had ever explicitly described the meal as a date.

He hadn't described it as anything at all.

Whatever John's feelings on the issue, they were soon forgotten as the quiet, and understandably sad, Mr Kwon explained the issue at hand.

A month earlier, his son's body had been found half-hidden by greenery beside The Cut – a cycle path that ran alongside the train line – not far from the station where Sherlock and John had alighted an hour before. He'd apparently been hit by someone travelling on a bicycle, had suffered blunt trauma from the impact with the ground, and passed away sometime in the night from exposure. The deceased had been found in the morning by a commuter who'd noticed his shoes.

As he spoke Sherlock handed the file to John to look through. Mr Kwon didn't question this sharing of what turned out to be intimate details of his son's life with a stranger, which made John wonder how he'd been described to the man.

He wasn't a pathologist. Since he'd finished his medical training he had always tried to avoid his patients turning up dead, so he wasn't entirely sure what Sherlock wanted him there for, but he looked at the file all the same.

There were no photographs but someone had written up a detailed list of the young man's injuries—fractured skull; missing teeth; tire tread pattern bruises across the chest; broken ribs; gravel burn. It all looked consistent with being hit by a bicycle.

'What did the police find?' Sherlock asked Mr Kwon while John turned to the next page which described the position of the body.

'Nothing. They looked at the station security camera footage, and we asked the businesses along Coombe Road to share theirs, but there wasn't much to go on. There's a few different places that a cyclist can join that path and most of them are residential. Whoever hit him might never have used the main road. Even if they did…' Mr Kwon sighed and shifted uncomfortably in his chair. 'I don't know how long my son was lying there, Mr Holmes. Dozens of cyclists use that route. I have to assume he was hit in the dark or they would have stopped and helped him. He was breathing.'

Just next to John's thumb was a description of the misted blood on the foliage inches from where the body was found. He'd definitely breathed his last there, rather than the body being moved.

'Not everyone is so considerate,' Sherlock said.

Just because the statement was true didn't make John want to slap him any less. He wondered if Sherlock spoke to all his potential clients like that.

Mr Kwon made a noise of distress but set his jaw all the same. He looked like a man who'd cried all the tears he had left.

'Wouldn't that make it murder, then?' he asked.

Sherlock shrugged. 'I don't know, I'm not a lawyer, it would doubtless depend on the circumstances.'

'Look, I just want justice for my son. Whatever a lawyer calls it – he was hit by someone and left to die. That should not have happened. The police say they can't identify any suspects from the video because the quality isn't good enough. I know you can do better. Please.'

'Leave it with me,' Sherlock said, then glanced at John, 'with both of us. We'll do what we can.'

John would have objected at that point, or at least asked whether he got a say in being involved in this investigation, but Sherlock had already put the money for the meal on the table and was walking out of the restaurant before he could even open his mouth to speak.

Unsure what to do, John picked up the folder of notes, nodded to the restaurant owner, and hurried after Sherlock. It was starting to become a habit.

'Do you always ask grieving parents to pay you in food, or was that just the deposit and you charge them cash?' John asked, once he'd caught up with Sherlock's long strides. His leg was aching but righteous anger made it a little easier to catch up.

'Do I look like a charity?' Sherlock snapped without slowing. If anything he seemed to be quickening his pace.

'Right now you look like a prick.'

Suddenly Sherlock stopped and turned into John's path, forcing them to collide though he caught John's arm before he could topple backwards into the street.

'No. I don't usually let people buy me meals for cases involving deaths, I tend to leave that for actual business cases which is how this was presented to me in the original email.' He'd started out angry but his words trailed off until he was staring into the distance. He didn't seem to be sure.

'Well, it wasn't presented to me like this. I'm not a monster. Do people who can afford it pay for my services? Yes. Because this is my job, John. You weren't in Afghanistan as a volunteer. No doubt some people are, and maybe there are people like me who can afford to work for free, but I am not one of them and neither were you.'

John felt his face twitch in distaste. He'd helped plenty of people out there without asking for payment, but he'd still been paid by the Crown for his 'day job'.

'And if people can't afford to pay you?'

'If they have an interesting enough case then they don't. Why do you think I need a flatmate?'

'You never asked me to be your flatmate!' John hissed through gritted teeth. 'I was moved in with you by the police!'

'And yet you never left, and you've been paying for your room since the second week of your stay,' Sherlock replied, stepping closer. 'Why are you angry about this, John? I paid for the meal. It was a misunderstanding. You knew my work when we started... whatever this is. I do my job and I do it well, but I have bills like anyone else.'

John stared at the pavement between their feet and forced himself to follow the red hot ball of anger in his gut back to its source.

'You made it sound like I was part of your *business*,' he said, at last, 'you didn't even ask me if I wanted any part in taking money from a grieving parent to investigate the death of their child. You just handed me the papers and expected me to follow.'

He didn't look up but he heard Sherlock swallow.

'I asked if you were free, John.'

'That isn't the same. You know that.'

'I won't charge him for this case. Is that what you want?' Sherlock sounded ashamed, and genuinely unsure.

'It would help, but...I don't know if I want to be involved in any of this. I'm a doctor. I deal with the living.' A dozen guilty memories from his childhood rose up then and tried to drag him down a path he didn't want to follow. 'I need a minute.'

'John, I...' Sherlock's shoes shifted awkwardly for a moment, then a warm hand squeezed John's bicep. 'Okay. I'm going to call the pathologist, see what she can tell me. Why don't you, I don't know, take a walk or something, to calm down?'

He nodded, and kept his eyes on the ground while the documents were slipped gently out of his hand before Sherlock walked away.

The street wasn't all that busy, but John walked on anyway. He was feeling self-conscious and not all that keen on being looked at right now. Probably no one *was* looking at him, but his skin prickled with discomfort all the same.

John followed the streets without really considering where he was going, choosing not to think about anything until his heart rate had slowed enough for rational thought.

'Whoa! Careful, dude!'

The shout made him look up, which meant that he stopped less than five feet from walking into the descending red and white pole of the level crossing.

How far had he walked that he'd made it back to the railway line? And how had he missed the flashing warning lights?

'You nearly got yourself hit by a train there,' the young Korean man who'd shouted him to a halt said with a grin. 'Now that would have been embarrassing.'

'Yeah,' John agreed, with a sheepish smile of his own. 'Thanks.'

But his saviour wasn't looking at him any more. Instead he was staring intently down the track at the oncoming train. Despite his fashionable-looking clothes, there was a small notebook in his hand and a pencil hovering just over the page.

John snorted to himself, half amused and half embarrassed by his own assumptions.

As the train roared past the young man carefully noted down the details and then finally looked at John again.

'Yeah, yeah, I'm a teenage railfan, I'm sure it's fucking hilarious, but at least I didn't nearly wander onto the line.'

'I didn't say anything,' John replied, noting the new term for *trainspotter*. He tried to make his expression neutral but he was pretty certain it didn't work from the glare he was getting. 'Thanks for saving me from an embarrassing death. I guess if I'd have been hit by the train it would have made the number harder to read.'

'Nah, I'm pretty sure I could've read it before it hit you,' he laughed and slipped the book into his back pocket. He shook his head ruefully. 'No worries, mate, I fell over the bike rack at the station last month. Too busy texting to see it. Just went arse over tit and smashed my head on the kerb. Thank fuck no one saw me before I got myself up.'

John blinked at him. His initial embarrassed glance and amusement at seeing the notebook had kept him from seeing the important details in the man's appearance.

There had been no pictures in the file of documents he'd been given, but the face in front of him had the same jawline as the restaurant owner and the beginnings of the same laughter lines that had turned to deep marks of sorrow on the older man's face. John looked at him, really looked at him, and finally noted the imprint of a bicycle tire on the left side of his shirt, the bruising on his face and the remnants of blood on his lower lip.

'You fell over the bike rack?' John asked. 'At New Malden station?'

'Yeah, but it was dark and that thing hasn't got flashing lights on it.' He laughed, pointing up at the sign John had failed to see beside the barriers. Just then the lights stopped. A second later the barrier began to raise. 'See ya!'

'Wait!' John called after him as he walked away, but an impatient pedestrian shoved past him and momentarily blocked his way.

By the time John had a clear view of the road again, the self-described 'railfan' was gone. Instinctively John knew that there was absolutely no point going looking for him.

Instead he stopped a safe distance from the railway line and dialled Sherlock's number.

Present Day – York

John had never told Sherlock exactly where he'd gotten the solution to *their* first 'official' case from – he had just said that a pedestrian had mentioned noticing a man fall.

Of course, Sherlock would always have noticed the shadowy corner of the security camera footage that the police had dismissed. When he insisted it be enhanced they found that it did in fact show the accident itself. The police had originally dismissed the slightly staggering figure that headed to The Cut on foot, but a tooth Sherlock found in a drain near the station matched with the son's dental records.

The coroner had agreed with Sherlock's assessment from there – it had been late at night. In the confusion of a head injury Mr Kwon's son had wandered away from any possible source of help and collapsed in the undergrowth by the cycle path without a witness.

Could John have told that quietly grieving father than his son seemed happy continuing to enjoy the trains that passed by?

No. It would not have helped. But he could tell him that he had gone peacefully, and no one else was to blame for his death.

The skull fracture had been severe enough that there had probably been no surviving it even if he had been found. As it was it seemed that he had fall asleep in the greenery near the train line and simply never woke up.

They'd been paid to deliver that news. John had felt sick even as the cheque was pressed into his hand with words of gratitude.

Sherlock had offered to donate it to some charity or other, reluctant not for reasons of greed but practicality.

There was good in Sherlock's work whether it brought justice or peace of mind, but there was also a cost to it.

G. V. PEARCE

In the end the money had been spent on rent and the things Sherlock needed to continue his work. All their money had been spent on that, it always was, but John had vowed to supplement it as much as he could.

Sherlock's cases had become *their* cases, just as Sherlock's bed had become *their* bed, John's heart had come to belong to Sherlock, and John had worked for the sake of Sherlock's work.

That finally was the real issue laid bare.

He was weary. He had two careers: Sherlock's and his own. It wasn't sustainable.

John watched the path of the river and knew why his heart was aching. He'd changed his life for Sherlock Holmes, but how much had Sherlock changed for him?

Never mind that John had come back from Afghanistan with little more than his medical qualifications and a leg that still ached in the cold. John had nothing, but he'd still given everything for the man beside him.

And Sherlock was still lying to him.

'This was supposed to be a substitute honeymoon,' he said flatly, his eyes still on the river and the space on the bench between them feeling like a million miles of solid rock.

'That's what you sold it to me as – a holiday. A goddamn break from everything. And what do I find here? Every-fucking-thing. Digging through visitor books, tramping through archives, literally taking apart museum displays. This is work. I knew on the train here that you were up to something and I went along with it, just like I always do.'

'Sorry.'

It was a quiet word that almost got lost in the rustle of the trees. But the word was there all the same.

Sometimes an apology is a good place to start.

Chapter Twelve

Present Day – York

Rain started to fall then, the first great fat drops of an early autumn downpour. Sherlock had taken his hand like nothing angry had ever been said between them and dragged John on a hurried dash to the nearest pub for shelter.

They tumbled through the door with three dozen other tourists, all laughing and soaked to the skin, too surprised by the rain to have time to get upset about it.

Sherlock looked particularly ridiculous. His usually neat hair had been ruined by the rain and was now hanging in dripping strands all around his face while Gloria's plastic-wrapped book was held protectively against his chest.

Despite himself John couldn't resist the urge to kiss him before he pushed him away to find a table.

From the quiet little park back into the bustle of the city centre was a shock to his system, but John was pleased that he managed to keep his wits about him enough to buy a couple of pints. He didn't really notice what kind of beer he'd bought; it was wet and something to do with his hands.

They had to talk.

Sherlock seemed to realise that too. He'd found them a booth hidden away in a corner, half concealed by a staircase and far too atmospheric for John's current mood.

Still, John didn't argue the point.

They sat in the shadows, staring at each other for what seemed like an age; John drawing idle patterns in the condensation on his glass, Sherlock alternately shaking back his wet hair and smoothing the plastic wrapping across the front of Gloria's book.

'Why didn't you just tell me this was work?' John asked.

The silence he'd broken seemed determined to reform like ice crystals around Sherlock's angular frame, so John asked again. 'Why did you lie to me?'

Sherlock didn't entirely meet his eye as he replied, 'I thought you'd say no.'

John laughed but didn't get a chance to comment; Sherlock cut off the bitter sound with an explanation.

'You never seemed all that comfortable with this case – her flat upset you, her books upset you, the clients upset you.'

'That's never stopped you before!' John realised he was almost shouting and took a gulp of his beer just to force his tongue to stop moving.

'It has, though!' Sherlock snapped back. Like John he stopped himself, pushing his fingers back through his hair and pulling on the ends with a little too much force. He didn't continue until he'd schooled his expression into something resembling calm.

'Look, I don't bring you into every case I get. Even if I didn't want to avoid upsetting you, you just don't have time to keep up with me on everything.'

That was all news to John. Yes, of course there had been nights when he'd returned from one extra long shift or another and Sherlock hadn't been there, but John had always thought that Sherlock was working on existing cases. How much was he keeping from him?

'We never talked about this,' John said in as neutral a voice as he could muster. 'What am I supposed to do if you just vanish one day?'

Sherlock sighed again and stared off into the distance. Serious discussion didn't come easily to either of them.

'I'm just, I'm not saving the dangerous cases for myself or anything...' he began, then trailed off.

'Yeah, well, that's patently obvious!' John said when it became clear that Sherlock had stalled again. There'd been more than enough dangerous cases. 'You certainly could have saved Dartmoor for yourself–'

'Dartmoor was a mistake—'

'You're right there!'

They stopped. They were half standing, leaning across the table like they were both ready to grab the other by the collar.

'This isn't us,' John said. He collapsed into his seat and ran his hands over his face in the hope that the sensation would calm him.

'I don't usually bring you in on the cases where loneliness and isolation play a part,' Sherlock said as he sank back into his own seat. 'I try to avoid the things that might remind you of before. You're not—'

'Right in the head? That'd be accurate.' John realised his voice was too snide. He raised his glass again. It was already half empty.

'This isn't *your* job, John, you don't *have* to do this—'

'And you do?'

'Please let me speak.' Sherlock sounded more resigned than sad now. He waited until John waved his hand to signal agreement before he continued. 'My point was that you could do this as a full-time job with me, and we'd make the money work somehow; or you can keep doing your own work, that you enjoy even if it burns you out from time to time, and you let me choose what cases we work on together.'

It was a good point but it wasn't *the* point right now. The point right now, right this second, was this case and this so-called holiday.

'This,' John tapped the book that was just peeking out from under Sherlock's hands, 'this is still work.'

'I thought you wouldn't notice,' Sherlock began, then changed tack when John's expression soured. 'Okay, I thought I wouldn't actually find anything. I swear I was just as surprised as you when one of Gloria's diaries turned out to be in the museum. She'd mentioned York a lot in the other volumes. I'd seen the photograph of her standing by the lockers online, plus there was a mention of the bag in the museum directory. Those were two of the very few results for her. The local paper had digitised the old photograph for a retrospective so I knew it was actually her. I couldn't not ask about the bag.'

'And what about that medieval charity?'

'That was another place she'd mentioned in her diaries, if only briefly.' He looked down at the book he was still compulsively smoothing with his fingertips. 'She had an interest in medieval religious art. I wanted to see if she'd made a donation that would help pinpoint when she was in the city. I needed more data for the next step.'

'Which is?' For all that Sherlock claimed not to be expecting anything from his searches he seemed to have had a plan in place all along.

'Well, it *was* going to be emailing all the local solicitor's offices in the hope that one of them might have documents that she'd paid for them to hold until they were informed of her death, however,' Sherlock paused to rummage in his pocket, 'I did find this amongst the receipts in the bottom of her bag.'

The thin slip of paper Sherlock placed on the table turned out to be a carbon copy of some kind of receipt. Across the top of the page was the printed name and address of a solicitor's office. Most of the blue pigment of the copied words had faded away, though the writer had pressed hard enough that most of the pen indentations were still legible.

'Last Will and Testament,' John read, 'something of July, 1983.'

'Looks like a three,' Sherlock said helpfully, then turned his head, 'or maybe an eight.'

'I doubt the precise day makes much of a difference.'

John watched as Sherlock carefully unwrapped the book that he'd taken from the museum. Sometimes John was still surprised by the things Sherlock could get away with just by turning on the charm. Then again, most people wouldn't even ask to borrow a museum exhibit in the first place.

He raised his glass only to find it empty. When did he drink the second half? He didn't remember.

That was how serious conversations with Sherlock usually went. Whatever John had planned to say would be swept away by Sherlock's focus on something else, and in the end John's curiosity would always allow the change in focus. Just like now.

'You just said you weren't expecting to find anything, and yet you knew she was going to leave documents?' John couldn't keep the resignation out of his voice while he watched Sherlock carefully turning the pages past the familiar sketches of the Minster.

'She didn't really mention her illness in detail in what I read. She was matter of fact about it but she didn't seem to be planning for…' He trailed off, not entirely sure that he could know anyone well enough from one book and a brief but awkward visit to their abandoned flat.

'You fell asleep, remember? After I found her diaries? She had a plan for life, things she did around work – charity, community, education – but she also had a plan for her own death. I think even before she became sick she was aware that she was alone. She knew she'd have to do something to set her affairs in order because no one else would do it for her.'

Sherlock abruptly stopped speaking and looked up at John with shining eyes. 'I really am sorry. I'll find the solicitor's current phone number, we'll sort out a visit as soon as possible, and then this holiday is ours. I promise.'

He honestly did look ashamed of himself, which had never been John's intent. Well, maybe a little. Or a lot. Sherlock did run roughshod over their lives at times. It wouldn't harm him to stop and think for a while. But John knew he should do the same.

'Sherlock, we've stopped and started this case half a dozen times,' John exaggerated as he reached out to grip Sherlock's hand across the open pages of the book. 'You know you want to see it through to the end. For whatever reason you think this is important. I don't necessarily disagree. I…'

There was a comforting squeeze on John's fingertips and he suddenly wished the table wasn't between them any more. Sherlock seemed to agree. He shuffled along the leather of the booth seat toward him and John followed suit. He'd forgotten they were even in a booth and that the separation between them was entirely artificial and unnecessary.

There was a metaphor in there somewhere but he couldn't be bothered to work it out.

His hip collided with Sherlock's own. The welcome impact was enough to tip him against Sherlock's side. John shivered with happiness as Sherlock turned at the touch to press his lips to any part of John's face that he could reach.

Eyes closed to better enjoy the attention, John continued speaking as soft chaste kisses rained down on his cheek and temple.

'I respect Gloria as a person, I think her diaries are a window into a different life and perhaps she should be published, but mostly I just wanted her to be left in peace. If you're telling me that tracking down her will or her next of kin is part of setting her to rest then I will follow you. But *please*,' John turned more fully in his seat to catch Sherlock's face in his hands. 'Don't do this again.'

Sherlock's eyes wandered for a moment, as if they were unwilling to meet John's gaze.

A gentle kiss fixed the problem. 'I'm serious.'

'John–'

'I didn't realise that you thought I was that bad,' John said. Part of him had foolishly expected Sherlock to agree right away, and now he was stuck trying to keep his frustration in check. 'I don't recognise your assessment of my mental state, and I don't know who is right on that topic, but I don't want you to treat me differently. I don't want you to make unilateral decisions about *our* lives.'

'What if I need to protect you?'

John waved a hand at the book still sitting in front of them. 'From a woman who's been dead for decades? I don't think she can do me any harm.'

'I don't mean...' Sherlock closed his mouth with a click as John pressed their foreheads together.

'I was a soldier, Sherlock, I have been shot, and I have been blown up, and I have saved lives in conditions you can't even imagine. I do not need protection.'

It wasn't until he finished speaking and Sherlock carefully took hold of his wrists that he realised he was trembling.

'What about government cases? Official secrets and need-to-know information?' Sherlock asked earnestly. 'What about when I don't have a choice?'

That, at least, was a valid point.

'But that's not about protection, that's following the client's guidelines, and when have you ever done that? I mean, really, actually done entirely as they've asked?'

Sherlock's serious expression melted into a devious smile. 'I suppose we could...devise a signal? Something that says I'm on a case I *legally* can't talk about, and then you can go along with it until I give in and tell you anyway?'

'Hah!' John laughed and kissed those perfect lips. 'The detective's equivalent of hanging a sock on the doorknob.'

That made Sherlock shake his head in mock disgust. 'I'm being serious.'

'Are you?'

'No.' He picked up his pint then drained it in one long motion that had John's eyes fixated on his throat, tracing the flow of every swallow.

Unable to keep his mouth shut at the sight John muttered, 'Beautiful.'

'Yes, darling?' Sherlock replied with a grin, but John only blushed and looked away. 'Come on. Let's go back to the guest house and call this solicitor.'

There were other things John would rather have done at the guest house, but he did want this holiday to himself, too, so he agreed. Perhaps he could get Sherlock into bed afterwards.

The solicitor's office turned out to be in a village about eight miles upriver from the city, and by the time Sherlock found a working telephone number it also turned out to be closed for the night.

Sherlock took this discovery as something of a personal affront to his methods. He was used to London, and London never slept. There was always a way to reach someone if necessary, especially when the caller was Sherlock Holmes, and so it came as a minor shock for him to learn that he couldn't always get what he wanted.

Most people learned this lesson by the age of five, but Sherlock never had, despite John's best efforts and constant frustration.

If John took a small amount of pleasure in Sherlock's upset he did also share some of his irritation on the matter. This was the last piece in whatever puzzle was being solved in Sherlock's head, and while he didn't actually believe that finding the solicitor would mean an immediate end to the case, he did want it to be over.

To fill the time until morning when they could sensibly leave for the village, they spent the evening wandering around the city, enjoying the cool air closer to the river until night fell and the street lights flickered on. The menacing atmosphere John had noticed in the morning faded with every street they walked down until ancient and modern standing side by side became a harmony instead of a discord in his mind.

Contrary to the prevailing folklore the ghosts who appeared to John rarely did so at night; or if they did, he noticed them less. Perhaps it was something of a cliché but the darkness seemed better suited to them, and so they were less jarring than in the cold light of day. Everyone saw odd shapes in the shadows so shadows were easy to dismiss. It was harder to ignore something he could see clearly.

The electric glow from the city hid the stars above them, just as it always did in London, but, John reflected, he'd never much needed the stars to navigate by. Certainly not now.

He turned to Sherlock with the intention of making some soppy declaration of love in which he compared the detective to his very own pole star like the lovesick idiot he apparently still was, but Sherlock wasn't there.

'Look, John!' He was standing at the other end of the picturesque alley, pointing at an A-frame sign that was half hidden amongst the shadows.

John frowned as he walked back to meet him.

Sherlock didn't often notice adverts, usually he was too busy thinking about more important things. Or at least things that Sherlock judged to be more important. That was a vital distinction that John had learned to make early in their relationship. Leaping out of bed at four in the morning could signal a breakthrough in a case, or just the sudden realisation that Sherlock didn't know what would happen if you set fire to a domestic kettle.

The sign appeared to be for one of the famous ghost-themed tours of the city. It promised a terrifying tour of all the city's most haunted places, starting in the Shambles – a famously narrow street that had once been home to the medieval city's meat trade.

'Didn't we walk that way earlier?' John asked. Suddenly he wasn't all that surprised at the dip in his mood. He didn't believe in 'negative energy' in a New Age kind of way, but the tiny portion of his psyche that acknowledged the things he'd seen over the years had to wonder if that much death could really leave a lasting impression on the place.

He tried to remember if he'd ever been to any of the old slaughterhouses in London. Of course, he'd never memorised all the details of London's history like Sherlock seemed to have done, so he had no idea.

Asking Sherlock about it was out of the question; he'd either get mocked or interrogated, and John was not in the mood for any of that nonsense tonight. He'd only made a few attempts at discussing the matter with anyone else. None of them had ended well. During his medical training and in the army he'd kept quiet out of fear of having his sanity brought into question. He'd lost several school friends before he learned that lesson; telling ghost stories was fun, claiming to have actually seen ghosts was 'mental'. Sherlock didn't believe in that kind of thing.

It didn't matter either way since Sherlock didn't hear him speaking; instead he had immediately launched into a series of his own, blessedly rhetorical, questions.

'Why do people believe in ghosts? I mean, all the 'evidence' for them can be disproven with the barest application of logic.'

Beside him John bit his tongue and gently slipped his hand

through Sherlock's arm. When he got into these moods it was best to ignore the ranting. If he could just remove Sherlock from the source of irritation they'd be just fine.

'I can slightly understand people believing these things before cameras were invented but really, how credulous do you have to be?'

'Come on,' John said, as soothingly as he could. 'We've got a long day tomorrow.'

Present Day – Monkton, North Yorkshire

If one were to take the idea of a bucolic English village, condense it down into its purest possible form, add an extra layer of wealth and a hint of threat, then wrap it all in a pleasant autumn day with just a suggestion of lingering sun, the mind would create an image of this village.

The place was so perfect it didn't even seem real. Walking down the main – and only – street, John got the impression that there was a camera crew hidden just outside the range of his vision. He wouldn't have been surprised if the picturesque buildings were actually nothing but set pieces. If a two-storey red brick house with roses around the door had blown over at that very moment to reveal the illusion of the place he probably wouldn't even have blinked.

There was a genuine village green surrounding a sizeable duck pond complete with willow trees and dozing swans.

A shining red telephone box stood in the middle of well-trimmed grass as if it had grown there like some kind of bizarre mushroom. Behind it stood a genuine Tudor coaching inn turned public house that seemed entirely at home juxtaposed with its slightly more modern brethren.

When he heard a car engine approaching John pulled Sherlock to the side of the road. A picturesque vintage Alfa Romeo trundled by them, so perfectly in keeping with the scene that John had to wonder whether it was real or an apparition.

He watched the car disappear between two lion-topped pillars into what seemed to be a private estate with a sense of irritation because he just couldn't tell.

Sherlock hadn't looked up, but that could have meant anything at all. Sherlock was the kind of man to ignore an explosion because he was too busy looking at a sandwich wrapper.

John had never personally seen a ghostly vehicle before – that he knew of – but he'd heard enough stories about spectral pirate ships and demonic cars to be suspicious.

He glanced around again. Wasn't there that one musical about an entire Highland village disappearing? What if Gloria had been spirited away by – no. There was an advertisement for this year's Premier League final in the pub window. He was getting carried away with himself.

The solicitor's office sat in the middle of a row of quaint shops, all beautifully maintained but sadly not yet open for the day.

Beside him Sherlock looked at his watch, looked at the sign on the door then intently stared at his watch again.

'Glaring at a time piece won't actually make reality run any faster,' John finally pointed out on the third iteration of the manoeuvre.

Of course, Sherlock already knew that but it was a choice between saying something and just slapping Sherlock's wrist.

John had mostly managed to restrain himself over the last few years, he wasn't going to break now.

'Pub?' he suggested.

Sherlock looked at him without understanding so John pointed the way across the green towards the building in question.

'Well done, John, you're right, that is, in fact, a pub.'

'I meant,' John said through gritted teeth, 'that we should go there. Like normal people. For a drink. While we wait.'

'Oh.' Sherlock looked at his watch again.

Two years of good behaviour be damned, John really was going to slap him in a minute.

'Fine!' Sherlock cried with enthusiasm just when John had given up any hope of getting a response.

Before John could even respond Sherlock had linked their arms and set off across the grass.

'Let's go!'

Well, at least he might get a drink.

CHAPTER THIRTEEN

Present Day – Monkton, North Yorkshire

ALTHOUGH THE DARK WOOD AND WHITE PLASTER EXTERIOR WAS IN keeping with the rest of the village's carefully maintained aesthetic, the interior of the pub had definitely gone through a phase of attempted modernisation.

This was not the creepy unwelcoming public house from a million low-budget horror movies.

There was only so much a person could do with a listed building – and certainly this one looked old enough to have been given protected status – but what could be updated had been. The decor was bright and cheerful, with every surface shining with lacquer. There were copper table tops and gilt busts of incongruous African wildlife. Someone had wanted to open a trendy ale house but had found themselves running the only pub in the village.

At least the handful of regulars sitting by the windows were the same standard-issue occupants of small-town pubs and bars the world over – quiet old folks seeking company, determined day drinkers, and the local gossip waiting for something interesting to happen.

John noticed a representative of the last category sit up in his seat as he and Sherlock moved towards the bar. This seemed like the kind of village where daily life was pleasant but monotonous, and the arrival of two strangers would probably be discussed for a few days, at least.

Based solely on the decor, John knew that the barman would have an impressive beard and a plaid shirt before he even stepped out of the kitchens to greet them, and he smiled to himself as he was proved right.

Although John would have always called his own style of dress 'generic,' Sherlock's love of old fashioned or vintage clothes would normally have made him a little unusual in most everyday settings. Here he unintentionally toed the line between the classic country clothing of the regulars and the deliberately fashionable choices of the barman.

John had never been entirely sure whether Sherlock was intentionally following modern trends or if it was just a coincidence that he blended in so well with the hipster crowd, but either way the effect worked in his favour.

The barman grinned at Sherlock like a friend he hadn't made yet.

'Fresh blood!' He laughed heartily though John didn't see a joke in the comment. 'Welcome to The Surgeon's Arms.'

Ah, well, that explained it. John hadn't even noticed the sign. He wondered if the name was traditional, but he wasn't curious enough to ask.

'What can I get you, chaps?' the man continued a little awkwardly when neither of the newcomers laughed with him.

Looking down the length of the bar John was dismayed to see an array of at least two dozen beers he didn't recognise. For most of them he didn't even recognise the brewery.

Sherlock, a man who rarely paid attention to what he ate and drank unless it had been introduced to him by a client, looked at John with an expression that begged for a rescue. All John could do was shake his head as subtly as he could; he was just as lost as Sherlock.

Finally, the instinct to charm that always served Sherlock so well reasserted itself. He smiled his most pleasant smile and asked in a tone that suggested he was speaking to a world expert, 'What would you recommend?'

From the other side of the room one of the regulars shouted, 'Two pints of whatever's most expensive!' but the barman just ignored him.

When John finally gave up and took a seat ten minutes into the barman's earnest lecture on the comparative qualities of different strains of barley, he wished he'd just picked a beer at random. Even though it wasn't relevant to the case the science of beer had apparently captured Sherlock's imagination, so now he was happily engaged in this fascinating discussion while his husband slowly died of thirst.

Well, that was an exaggeration of course, but John felt strange to be sitting in a pub without any kind of beverage in front of him.

A movement at the corner of his vision made him look up just in time to see another man drop into the seat across the table. It was the one who'd sat up in interest when he and Sherlock had arrived, the one John had assessed as the local gossip.

'Morning,' the man said in an accent so broad that John was already worrying that he wouldn't understand him. Before John could respond the man tipped his glass to him and introduced himself. 'I'm Jeff. You lads out here for the camping? It's getting to be a bit off season for it now, but there's some good fishing out there if you don't pay no mind to the stories.'

John glanced at Sherlock in the hope of getting some kind of assistance but he'd progressed to peering into shot glass samples of beer with the enthusiastic barman. Aid would not come from that quarter.

'We're here for the solicitor,' John said flatly. Perhaps if he made this conversation uninteresting it would end sooner.

'What, old Barraclough? I'm always amazed when he manages to totter down to his office every morning, he's got to be ninety if he's a day.' Jeff shook his head in disbelief, then took a sip of his beer. 'Course he's been here as long as anyone can remember so probably can't even die at this point. He's a, what do you call it, an institution, that's it.'

Jeff continued speaking before John could even formulate a reply. 'O' course, he hasn't been the same since the summer of '83, but then who can blame him?'

Instead of replying John just waited for him to go on, and like an automaton in an interactive museum he did just that.

'There's good fishing up by the campground,' Jeff repeated, 'at the bend in the river. Lots o' chub and roach and barbel. One of the local lads caught a seventeen pound salmon up there in '84, it were bloody amazing.'

'We're not here to fish,' John said in a futile attempt to stop the monologue.

'That were after the accident, though, if you believe it even happened. Personally, I ain't sure, though there's stories enough, right through to only last month. Cormack over there says he saw it when he was out night fishing, didn't you, Cormack?'

Jeff pointed to an old man who seemed to have sunk down into his unseasonably heavy coat like a tortoise into its shell. At the sound of his name he retreated further until only his nose was visible through the gap of his collar.

'Mad old bastard, but a good 'un,' Jeff muttered into his pint glass as he raised it to his lips again.

John was starting to get the impression that despite the decor, he had actually walked into the beginning of a certain type of horror film. Wasn't this how they always started – some creepily intense local gleefully recounting the history of the moors to a pair of oblivious tourists who would inevitably wander into their own doom?

This was the point where John was supposed to ask for an explanation of the vague hints and insinuations. As he replayed the man's words his brain tripped over a date.

'Wait, what was that about 1983?' he asked. Hadn't Gloria been here that summer?

Jeff's grin at the question couldn't have got any wider without the top of his head falling off.

'Well,' he said with far too much glee in his voice.

Summer, 1983 – River Ouse, North Yorkshire

The summer of 1983 had seen a mixture of storms, high humidity and – for England – extreme heat. Across the country there were reports of the heat overwhelming public services, with rivers running dry, and chaos on the roads as overall temperatures reached the highest level in centuries.

Here in the village things had continued much as normal. The local children ran wild in the nearby fields where the grass yellowed under the hot sun and adventure seemed to be waiting around every corner. For the adults the days crawled by while every evening the pub did record trade as the beer garden filled with thirsty locals and the small influx of tourists who preferred quiet rural landscapes to busy beaches and run-down coastal holiday camps.

Jeff had been a teenager then, just old enough to be preoccupied by thoughts of his own future but still tempted by the folly of youth.

As the temperatures soared Jeff and his friends searched for any kind of relief, no matter how dangerous.

The village was ten miles from the city and even further from the nearest swimming pool, but the river, well, that was right there on their doorstep.

Hadn't they grown up with the river? Played on the banks, joined in with the fishing, paddled in the shallows?

Did it really matter that they weren't the strongest swimmers when they'd known this stretch of cool, refreshing water their entire lives?

Jeff himself only had pleasant memories of the river.

The campground ran alongside it, the bank wide and grassy, and, most importantly, open to the sun. So many girls had sunbathed there. Jeff had spent just as much of his summer watching them from the relative comfort of the cool, deep river.

There were always younger kids hanging around, but Jeff had paid them no mind. Apparently, no one had, and so no one really knew what had happened that particular day.

Here Jeff had segued into an inappropriate aside about where he personally had been that night, and John was forced to cut off the reminiscing before he learned more than he wanted about the man's teenage sex life.

No one was quite sure when the Barraclough kids – the three grandchildren of the local solicitor – had wandered away from the pub where their family were enjoying the cool evening air, but it was their mother who first noticed their absence, just after sunset.

A search was still being organised when someone came running from the direction of the campground screaming for a doctor.

The youngest Barraclough child – a little girl aged about four or five – had been found half drowned and unconscious on the bank of the river. The other two were found further downstream a short while later, in a similar condition.

As local dramas went it was a good one, and the incident would have been a topic for gossips regardless, but it was the children's story that cemented it into something of a legend.

They'd gone to the river, they said, at sunset to avoid the adults that might have told them not to go into the water. At that time of the evening the sunbathing spot was deserted except for one figure laid in the grass. The woman had seemed to be asleep.

It had been the middle child, a sickly girl of eight who was the first to get into difficulty in the water. Where it bent the river sometimes formed a whirlpool and she had been dragged down by it. Her little sister had leapt into the water with the bravery of all tiny children, absolutely confident that she could save her. Realising the disaster before him, the boy had followed without ever even thinking to get help.

Looking back, the children said they believed they had woken the woman sleeping on the bank with their shouting because she had suddenly been in the water with them. They described her as skinny but strong, and each of them independently said that she had hauled them out of the water as best she could before returning for the rest.

Unfortunately, there was a three day delay between the drama and the children being well enough to give a statement.

The police found no trace of the woman. There was no tent, caravan or car left behind and no witness had seen her, but the police had searched the shoreline for miles downstream just in case. They recovered nothing during their search, and the general opinion was that the children had invented her.

The children's grandfather – the lawyer John and Sherlock were waiting to meet – had been deeply offended by the accusation, and had defended their version of events ever since.

Still, the story might have been forgotten if a visiting angler hadn't shown up in the pub three years later dripping wet and claiming to have been rescued by a shadowy figure.

He wasn't the only one – there had been a dozen near drownings in the last three decades, and all of them had ended with a mysterious rescue.

Behind the bar a stylised clock chimed the hour and Jeff sat back in his chair with the air of a master storyteller.

John frowned and asked quietly, 'So the woman came back? For years? That seems unlikely.'

'No, she's a bloody ghost!' Jeff cried, but all the wind was knocked out of his sails when John met his dramatic expression with only his blandest stare.

John didn't need to be convinced of the existence of ghosts.

'Of course,' Jeff muttered, 'I nearly drowned in that river myself, back in '08, and no ghost ever tried to rescue me.'

His pouting was interrupted when Sherlock reappeared empty handed from the bar.

'Time to go,' he said. 'We can come back and get a beer later if the barman can find one that doesn't taste entirely of chemicals.'

John turned back to Jeff to apologise for his husband's rudeness, but the other chair was empty. He glanced around but there was no sign of Jeff anywhere. No even an empty pint glass.

Across the room the locals were staring at him again.

He felt sick. How long had it been since he'd made the mistake of speaking to a dead person in front of witnesses?

He'd learned that lesson with the cat, more or less. As a young teenager he'd found safety in numbers. If ghosts usually manifested when he was alone then he had tried not to be alone in public. The sports clubs and occasional lads' night out had given him a reputation for being sociable despite the long hours he'd dedicated to his education. To his knowledge no one had ever noticed that he always waited for someone else to do the introductions. Maybe they just thought he was oddly formal, which was definitely better than people thinking he was mental. The habit had faded as he aged but the embarrassment and guilt of being caught still rushed back just as clear as the day Henry told him off.

There was no way they were coming back to this pub.

Despite the previous unflattering description of the solicitor, Mr Barraclough was actually a relatively spry man of almost ninety. More the sort to take part in marathons until the day he died than a man who shuffled everywhere under the weight of the world. If he was carrying significant trauma, he was doing a fantastic job of hiding it.

Having explained his role, and shared what few credentials he had, Sherlock slid the receipt and one of the edited photos of Gloria across the desk along with copies of her birth certificate and passport.

'Hmmm,' Mr Barraclough said doubtfully after finding his glasses and studying the documents in detail. 'Well, yes, of course I do keep all the documents that are entrusted to me safe, but 1983… that's going to be something of a chore to find. You understand that for reasons of space we have to rearrange things from time to time.

'If she was born in 1946, she should be an advanced age by now, but you say you have reason to believe that she's dead. What evidence are you intending to submit? Depending on the circumstances I'm sure you understand that I can't just release the will to you.'

Sherlock nodded. 'Naturally. It may be that we simply ask you to contact her next of kin, if you have the information available, or we just advise the clients to have the Probate Service act as intermediaries in the settling of their own case.'

He looked at John then. John looked back, unsure why he was being looked at until Sherlock prompted him with the stress on his title, '*Doctor* Watson?'

'Oh, yes,' John said as he struggled to regroup. He'd expected Sherlock to explain what they had, but it was a natural assumption that a solicitor might put more weight on the word of a medical professional. 'We believe that your encounter with her was one of the last known instances of her having been seen alive. So far we haven't been able to trace her body, but we do know that she never returned to her property in London, and she was suffering from a terminal form of cancer at the time.'

Mr Barraclough's impressively thick white eyebrows raised at that. He picked up the photograph again.

'I think I remember her now,' he said in a vague tone of voice. 'Her hair didn't look like that, though.'

'She was carrying a selection of scarves with her,' John prompted. He recalled that detail from the list of items Sherlock had found in her bag. 'She might have had her hair covered?'

The solicitor nodded, his fingertip tapping out a syncopated rhythm against the edge of the photograph as he considered the matter.

'Hmmm. Yes. It was orange, or maybe lime green; no, perhaps it was both. Hmmm...' He trailed off.

After a breath or two his eyes began to close and John glanced at Sherlock. Had their witness just fallen asleep?

'Yes!' The word was so loud and unexpected that John actually jumped. 'Yes, I was confused because she came *back*. It was orange the first time and patterned the second, or maybe the other way around, but she was memorable because, well, her appearance was unusual for a rural village at the time. She came originally because someone in the city had mentioned the country house across the river – it had something to do with the American military during the war – but she somehow found herself on our side of the river instead. If I recall correctly, making her will here was a spur of the moment idea; she just happened to see the office and came in.'

'And she came back?' Sherlock asked. He looked almost nervous.

John couldn't help but wonder if Sherlock was worried that she'd taken the will away with her. If that was the case they'd almost certainly never find it.

'Oh, yes, I think she wanted to try the camping or something, we're famous for it around here.' Mr Barraclough's voice cracked as he spoke. He removed his glasses and rubbed at his eyes in a gesture that could have been read as tiredness or a cover for an emotional response. 'Sorry, I don't really recall very much about her second visit other than that it happened. It was a difficult period. A lot going on. Family, you know.'

The old man coughed then and stood with less ease than when he first greeted them, but his face was determined all the same.

'If you come back tomorrow I'll find the documents for you,' he said, both his tone and his had gesture pointing them towards the exit.

Chapter Fourteen

Present Day – Monkton, North Yorkshire

'I HATE YOU.'

'No, you don't,' Sherlock said cheerfully as he climbed over yet another root and turned back to offer a hand. 'You just hate some of the things I do, that's different.'

John rolled his eyes and sighed. 'Okay, fine. I hate myself for agreeing to any of this.'

He still didn't know quite how he'd ended up out here in the woods. As they'd left the solicitor's office Sherlock had turned to him and asked whether he liked camping. John had no strong opinion on it one way or another. He'd spent enough time sleeping under canvas in the army to know that he wasn't precious about it, but he did enjoy a real bed and a source of electricity so he couldn't exactly say he had a preference for it. Which had been a mistake.

Like any sane person John had assumed that he and Sherlock would be getting another taxi back to the city and the room they were already paying to use.

But he'd failed to account for Sherlock's spontaneous side. Multiple people had recommended the campgrounds and now he had it in his head that they should stay there. John had tried to dissuade him but he'd already known it was hopeless. Hell, a few weeks ago he had been unable to talk him out of climbing the roof of St Pancras Hotel; he'd have absolutely no chance of avoiding something as innocuous as a camping site.

Which was how he'd ended up here – staggering through a horribly dark woodland looking for a place that was allegedly ten minutes walk from the village.

The village they'd left just over three hours ago.

At least Sherlock was carrying the basic camping gear he'd thought to rent from the pub's barman, rather than just setting off and assuming they could rent something from the campground itself. Apparently since they'd just missed the end of the season there would be no one working there – unless there was an anglers' event going on – and therefore nothing to rent. They might even be alone there.

Regardless of the reassurance that they at least wouldn't be sleeping under the stars, John was still unhappy about the entire situation, not least because his leg was screaming at him. It had been for almost the entire time they'd been lost amongst the trees. Uneven ground was a pain in the arse to navigate at the best of times without getting lost, too.

Sherlock had offered to carry him, more than once and probably not in a joking way, but John could see that the pack on Sherlock's own back was beginning to bother his arm. There was no benefit in incapacitating them both. Besides, there was something undignified about being carried for long distances. It stopped being sexy after about a hundred feet and started to get a bit humiliating.

'Look, since we're going to be lost in here forever, and we're probably going to die in these woods, why don't you explain what you think you're going to find in that will?' John suggested. 'You know, to keep my mind occupied before the inevitable.'

Sherlock had walked ahead of him again, his long, healthy, and very attractive legs setting a pace John couldn't match on this terrain.

He almost thought that he hadn't been heard when Sherlock's shoulders shifted with the characteristic huff that signalled details being pulled from him against his will.

Why a man who loved the sound of his own voice so much insisted on that little performance John never knew, but it made him smile to see it. The melodrama was part of the charm, after all.

'We know her father was a GI,' Sherlock began, his eyes fixed on the shadowy path ahead. 'Well, we know that's what we were told. We know from the card she wrote to her mother – that we're supposed to think was torn up at the time – that her parents weren't able to marry one another, so they married other people. Presumably her mother married her stepfather after Gloria's birth. That's most likely given the time period. Some war babies were born to married women but Gloria specifically mentions her mother being a single parent for a while in her diaries, and I didn't find any mention of a wedding.'

The words wavered slightly as Sherlock negotiated a boggy patch of ground. 'And then we're meant to believe that her stepfather and her British half-siblings rejected all contact with her. Do you remember they said they'd never heard of her?'

He paused then to turn back to John with a look of apologetic skepticism. It was the look he wore whenever he was quoting a witness' less-likely statements. Sometimes John suspected Sherlock felt physical pain at repeating such nonsense.

'And yet there were sketches of the same children in every one of her diaries,' Sherlock continued as if that was the greatest revelation of the age.

'Well, those children weren't necessarily her relatives. Even if they were, maybe one of her siblings was racist even if the others weren't and that stopped the clients from ever meeting her,' John said, frowning as he tried to remember any details from the sketches.

The conversation was suddenly derailed when a tree root he would've sworn wasn't there a second ago jumped out and ambushed him. That was definitely it; it wasn't that he'd been too distracted to look where he was going.

Once Sherlock had hauled him back onto his feet they walked on in silence until John tripped again. This time he didn't fall but the shock of it irritated him.

'I don't think the camping site is haunted,' he griped, 'I think the campground *is* the ghost. Why would anyone even want to go on a haunted camping trip?'

Sherlock shook his head. 'It's the river that's supposed to be haunted.'

'Fine, who wants to go fishing for ghosts then?'

The woodland path was widening out now, the gaps in the trees turning brighter as more sun broke through the canopy.

Sherlock snorted, his eyes still dutifully fixed on the ground beneath his feet. 'Now, now, John, there's supposed to be good eating on a sole...Oh.' His smug laughter at his own pun trailed away when he finally looked up.

The campground was, for want of a better word, idyllic. Lush green grass as thick as carpet; trees with blossom that scattered in the breeze; the smells of loam, honeysuckle, and cool fresh water drifting through the warm air.

It was almost paradise.

But it was also late September.

'Correct me if I'm wrong, but climate-wise – this isn't right, is it?' John said slowly as he looked around.

He hadn't paid a great deal of attention in geography, but he knew enough to know this wasn't right. They had not been walking for long enough to justify this semi-Mediterranean climate, no matter what his knees told him.

The village had been green and idyllic but this was just uncanny. 'Sherlock?'

The only answer he got was a shrug. Of course, Sherlock rarely ventured out of London. While he'd probably be able to tell you the exact temperature differences in the microclimate around the Thames, he'd be hard pressed to find York on a map, let alone comment on its weather.

John stepped forward to walk around Sherlock and out onto the grass.

'Oh my.' It felt like the air had been knocked out of his lungs.

An overwhelming sense of peace washed over him, like being wrapped in an heirloom blanket made by a much-loved but now deceased relative. Comfort. Echoes of happy times. Not a reduction in pain but a sense of freedom from it. A lifting of grief. The sensation made his heart stutter in the strangest of ways.

When he looked at Sherlock he found the same look of surprise on his husband's face, for just an instant. Then Sherlock shook his head and the expression was gone.

The grass was warm under John's legs as he sat watching Sherlock set up camp.

They were alone, just as the barman had predicted they might be, and with all the open space to choose from Sherlock had spent a quite excessive amount of time deciding where to put their tent.

At first John had tried to help, but after the third rejected suggestion – complete with hand gestures to better support Sherlock's reasoning – he'd decided he'd rather sit in silence and avoid an all-out argument. He felt far too serene for that right now.

Staring at the sky he wondered whether he should be worried about the atmosphere here. The unseasonable weather could be put down to nothing more than a very sudden 'Indian summer'. It wasn't as if he and Sherlock actually followed the weather forecast all that much. Sherlock would certainly attribute the sensation of calm to low blood sugar or something.

Did it matter?

John flopped back to lay completely flat in the grass so he could watch the clouds drifting by in comfort.

Now this, this was a proper holiday.

He sighed and let himself relax, working though his muscles in stages from his toes to up to his neck. Had he realised how much tension he was carrying? Probably. He should ask Sherlock for a massage one day soon.

As if summoned by the thought he heard Sherlock call, 'Are you falling asleep over there?'

'Hopefully!' he shouted back. He didn't bother turning his head to look at him.

There was a muffled rustling, a thwack, and a grunt that suggested something delicate had been caught by a tent pole.

'Who'll rescue me if I lose the battle against this tent?' Sherlock asked. It was a plaintive kind of wail.

John laughed and draped an arm over his eyes. 'I'll bury you in the river with full military honours. It's like burial at sea but on an installment plan.'

The only response was a string of half-muttered swearwords that cut off with another thwack.

It wasn't a perfect peace but John was happy to take what he could get.

'John? Are you awake? John? *John! Jo...*'

'Yes! Damn it, I was never asleep!' he groaned. He wasn't entirely clear on that one but he wasn't going to admit it.

'I set up the tent. And I have food,' Sherlock said as he plopped down onto the grass at John's side.

Pushing himself up on wobbly arms John let his eyes follow Sherlock's hand toward the 'food'.

'This is a packet of crisps. One. One packet of crisps. Not one each. One.'

Sherlock stared at him with wide innocent eyes for a record twenty-two seconds before his expression crumpled into a grin. He could be a great actor when he really set his heart on it, but he always failed when it came to John.

'Don't worry, I've got scotch eggs and sausage rolls, too.' He emptied his pockets onto the grass between them, listing each item as it appeared. 'Pastries, and Cornish pasties, and I know I have a pork pie in here somewhere.'

John laughed and grabbed his arm. 'You got all this food just for today?'

'Yes. And a banana too since I know you'd complain about a lack of fruit if I didn't.'

That was definitely true. His very next comment would have been something about the overall healthiness of the food because he was a doctor and because Sherlock had been known to fixate on things to a ridiculous degree. Like that week he'd somehow eaten nothing but cooked smoked sausage. How he'd managed it was a mystery, and since he was an adult John never intended to nag but then Sherlock would do something...

He stopped that train of thought and kissed his husband instead.

'Are you okay, John?' The question was quiet and earnest, a tiny little sound whispered against his lips like Sherlock was worried about the squirrels overhearing them.

'Me? Yeah, I'm fine.'

A stock answer, given by rote without a thought.

Sherlock watched him seriously but John didn't know how to actually answer the question.

'Let's, uh, let's take the food down to the river,' he suggested in a statement so awkward he could feel every muscle in his body cringe at once. 'I haven't seen it yet.'

The campground was a lozenge shaped expanse of grass, bordered on the east by woodland and on the west by the curve of the riverbank. Here the water was at it widest with the other bank at least twenty metres away. At the apex of the curve on both sides there were sandy strips of exposed riverbed. Almost like sandbars at the coast.

He had to admit that the view was enticing. John could understand the temptation to walk out onto the sand or dive into the flat calm of the water.

Further down river – just before the water's course curved again and vanished from view – John could see that the stillness gave way to white tipped ripples and waves that pulled at the long reeds along the bank.

The view upstream was much the same.

Stooping slightly Sherlock gripped the sausage roll he'd been eating between his teeth to free his hands.

John frowned as he watched him pick up and reject half a dozen sticks before he finally found a willow bough that matched whatever exacting standards Sherlock had for tree branches.

With a surprising amount of grace Sherlock hurled it into the air towards the middle of the river.

The bough landed, drifted for a second and then spun in place.

They watched it, waiting for it to move on, but it didn't.

'Mrfph,' Sherlock said. He removed the half sausage roll from his mouth and tried again. 'Whirlpool. It looks calm but it isn't.'

'Huh.'

The branch spun on until John had to turn away. 'Okay, now I feel dizzy. I guess that explains why people keep getting into difficulties in there.'

Sherlock nodded. He touched John's arm with his free hand, the look of concern back in his eyes.

'I'm okay,' John said, dropping to ground to sit against the base of a tree that was still in the sun. 'Really. I am. I'm just...'

He stopped. He didn't even know himself.

In the pause Sherlock took the opportunity to sit down next to him. Their shoulders weren't quite touching.

The night before had been awkward. Walking so far across the unfamiliar city had taken its toll on John's body so that by the time they were getting ready for bed not just his leg but his shoulder had been on fire with pain. It came in waves and it came with contact. Sherlock understood, of course he did, but after such a serious discussion it had been uncomfortable for them both to sleep so far apart.

'You're not okay, are you?' Sherlock said. He was looking at the river still but John didn't mind. Right now eye contact felt like it would be too much.

John opened his mouth and the truth poured out. 'I'm tired, Sherlock. Literally. I'm just stretched too thin and there's never enough sleep in the world. I feel heavy and wrong, and I keep snapping when I don't mean to because I know you, so I know you don't mean to make...to make every damn thing so difficult.

'No. You see? That isn't what I meant. I just, bloody hell Sherlock, I just want to sleep and between jumping from job to job and case to case it feels like I never get a chance except – I also feel like I'm always sleeping. I can't keep up with you. You're like a shooting star flying across the sky and I'm just a kid who thinks that running across the grass means he can keep up with the light.'

He paused for breath fully aware that he wasn't making sense but without a single clue as to how to fix it.

Sherlock laid a cool hand on his forearm without a word. It felt like an anchor, not weighing him down without a reason but keeping him safe in a storm he couldn't entirely see.

'Are you ill?' Again the question was asked without eye contact but John could tell that Sherlock was looking at the places where his own hand met John's skin.

The truth could be terrifying, but it could also be freeing.

'I don't know,' John admitted. 'I could be burnt out. My depression might be manifesting in a different form, I might have a virus, I – I don't know. I thought I could assess myself. I've been keeping track of how I feel on my phone but that hasn't made anything clearer.'

It was a horrible thing to admit – as a doctor – that he had no idea what was going on. In a way his health was like Schrödinger's cat: if he never checked it out he'd never have to face a difficult diagnosis. Perhaps he was a coward, or maybe he was genuinely too busy to get it done, but the reasons didn't really matter, did they?

John wasn't sure quite when Sherlock had turned but he was looking at him now. His face was full of love with a hint of fear and just a tinge of reproach as he stated the obvious.

'You need to get some testing done. You need to see another doctor. Someone whose perception of 'normal' isn't as skewed as ours.'

'Yes,' John nodded.

'Do we cut this short? Go back to London today?'

That should have been a tempting offer but John shook his head. 'We're close to the end of our case. Once it's done, then we can decide.'

Sherlock's hand slid slowly down John's arm until he gently laced their fingers together.

'Ian and Jessica, our clients, are actually Gloria's half-siblings; not her niece and nephew,' he said suddenly. 'It took me a while to find them. Gloria's mother moved around a lot and remarried twice so the details on Gloria's birth certificate were only so much help.

'But I found birth certificates for Ian and Jessica Chilcote who were both born in the late '60s with the same mother as Gloria and a father called Brian.'

John frowned as he took a scotch egg from the pile Sherlock had reassembled between them. 'Why would they say they were her niece and nephew?'

'Well,' Sherlock said thoughtfully, 'they called Gloria both 'a relative' and 'an aunt', so it's possible that they were lied to about her identity. She was born after the war to an unwed teenage mother – a common thing for families to cover up back then. There was over fifteen years age difference between her and them, so it would have been easier to conceal the truth.'

He didn't look convinced, though, and John could feel his fingers tapping out some rhythm on the back of his hand while he spoke.

'Most of the children's portraits in her diaries had either an 'I' or 'J' doodled beside them, particularly the ones where they're babies and just look like Winston Churchill. But they were both quite old in the last sketch. Old enough that they should've remembered her. I think they did know her and they lied about it.'

'Why?'

Sherlock held up his hand, grimaced at the crumbs stuck to his fingertips, brushed them off, then raised a finger. 'One – I looked at the Bona Vacancia lists – I can't find the case number mentioned in the heir hunters' contract.'

Another finger raised. 'Two – they asked us not to contact the heir hunters about their case because it was a clear violation of the contract they hadn't even signed, but when I tried the number on the letterhead it was disconnected.

'Three – I did find an American Lieutenant Colonel Evans who passed away just over a year ago. I suspect that was Gloria's father.'

'Okay,' John said slowly. He was coming up blank on the name. 'Should I know who that is?'

'Probably not,' Sherlock admitted. 'He was well known in his own state for his wealth, political, and philanthropic work, but he wouldn't have been internationally famous. By the time Gloria wrote that card we reconstructed, he was already a millionaire. According to news reports, at the time of his death it was tens of millions.'

'Okay.'

John felt like a stuck record. The sun had finally vanished behind the trees. Even in a preternaturally lovely place like this, without the sun to warm it the air became noticeably cooler than when they arrived. He shifted slightly, triggering a rush of pins and needles down his leg.

He groaned and hauled himself upright. 'Let's get back to the tent. We should probably build a fire.'

'Already done,' Sherlock said, jumping up once John had moved away from the tree.

There was a flurry of activity as he returned the food to his pockets, then one long arm was wrapped around John's back in a supportive gesture that could easily be passed off as normal affection.

John was glad of that; he didn't need help walking back but it was nice to know that Sherlock was always there if he did need him.

'So,' John mused while they picked their way across the grass that was already beginning to glitter with dew. 'Are you saying this is an inheritance thing, but from the other side of the family? They're trying to get something from Gloria's father? But they *aren't* related to him, *and* she had six other half-siblings on his side – so they wouldn't be the ones to inherit, surely?'

Sherlock's smile was difficult to see in the twilight but John could feel his pleasure at the reasoning.

'Absolutely,' he said. 'But we do know that Gloria's flat was being paid for through a trust fund. I couldn't get any details on it at the time, but I wouldn't be surprised if the fund received some portion of that inheritance. And if Gloria died intestate–'

'Then her half-siblings here would inherit,' John said, finally starting to follow the logic. 'Wait, wouldn't all the siblings inherit?'

'Probably, though I believe some of them have died in the meantime. They were closer to Gloria's age than our clients are.' Sherlock made that same expression of distaste when he said 'clients.'

He clearly wasn't happy to be connected with them. 'But even an eighth of a fortune is better than nothing, plus there's the property to be sold. It needs work but other flats in that building have sold for half a million.'

'Hmmm.' John still wasn't sure.

'Perhaps they really did just want us to prove her death so they could inherit the flat – I've done that kind of work before. But there's got to be some reason for all this subterfuge.'

'Now *that* is true,' John laughed for a moment, then stopped when he realised they'd made it back to their own camp site.

To John's surprise Sherlock had actually collected a great deal of wood and arranged some of it in a circle of stones a safe distance from the tent.

While he set about lighting it John retrieved a couple of blankets. They smelled musty as he sat on one and wrapped the other around his shoulders, but so long as he was warm he really wasn't fussy about that kind of thing. Besides, the comforting smell of the campfire soon covered anything else.

That was until Sherlock joined him under the blanket and wriggled close to his side. Then John's nose was full of the old books and vintage clothes smell that seemed to follow him like a cologne. They'd been out in nature for most of the day but Sherlock still smelled like an ancient library.

John turned his head to press his nose against Sherlock's hair, breathing deeply.

CHAPTER FIFTEEN

Two Years Ago – Marylebone, London

THE FIRST TIME SHERLOCK HAD SHARED HIS BED THEY HADN'T EVEN been dating, though they had kissed three times at least. Not that John was in the habit of tracking such things but they had been wonderful kisses in their own right, twice as part of Sherlock's cover and once as themselves just before Sherlock climbed into John's bed with the stated aim of soothing his flashbacks.

John had laid there the next morning, just after 6am, wondering what to do next.

Normally, dating for him involved either awkwardly dancing around the issue with a lab partner until they got annoyed and kissed him first, or swiping through an app on his phone where he could be entirely confident of what the other man was looking for. He'd had some success with both, and he had had a few short to medium-term relationships before he joined the army. But with Sherlock he had to admit that he was a little bit lost.

Forgetting that the bed was only a twin, John had rolled onto his back – intending to stare at the ceiling for a while in case it could offer any advice on the situation – when the movement all but forced Sherlock out of the bed.

Sherlock must have been dozing. He'd definitely been awake when John fell asleep but when John moved Sherlock made a noise of panic and grabbed John with grip tight enough to bruise.

The manoeuvre was awkward in the narrow space but John managed to pull Sherlock back onto the mattress before he fell too far toward the carpet.

Now they were pressed chest to chest. John could feel Sherlock's rapid breathing against him, the firm warmth of his arms, the heat of his breath. He breathed deep, trying to calm his own racing heart at the contact.

Sherlock was still half asleep; now was not the time to get excited. All the comments of the night before might have been said just to reassure him, or Sherlock might have been confused by waking up to John's screaming. Either way there was no guarantee Sherlock really wanted to date him.

Sherlock's lips found his mouth.

This kiss, the fourth of their not-quite-a-relationship, was soft but determined. What started as chaste, almost imperceptible touches against his skin turned into gentle nips of his lower lip with a soothing tongue that followed every bite.

John hesitated. It was so much harder to resist when he was actively being kissed – but Sherlock was asleep.

Almost as if he'd heard his thoughts the man opened his eyes.

They were pressed so close together that Sherlock's eyelashes fluttered against John's skin. He broke the kiss with an undignified giggle, then blushed and ducked his head in embarrassment.

Sherlock smelled amazing. It was a ridiculous thought to have in this situation, but with his face all but nuzzled up against his neck, John found that he couldn't resist the urge to breathe deeply and enjoy it all the more.

'Are you sniffing me?' Sherlock murmured as he turned his own head to kiss along John's jawline.

'No.' John meant 'yes' but he was unwilling to admit it as he took another deep breath. 'You smell good,' he continued, immediately disproving his own denial.

'I'll take that as a compliment.'

'Good,' John said, finally leaning back. 'What are we doing?'

Sherlock tipped his head in confusion. 'Making out?'

Well, technically that was the correct answer but John hadn't meant the question like that. But his brain was still barely awake.

Perhaps it was something in his face or just Sherlock's superior skill at understanding the most tenuous of clues but he seemed to understand the question John was failing to ask.

He ran his fingers back to John's hair, gently encouraging him to raise his head so their foreheads rested together. As he spoke his hand stayed in John's hair as a warm, soothing weight.

'I'm kissing you because I want you. You fascinate me.'

'You're hardly here,' John interrupted, surprised by the confession.

'I have no cases right now, I could take a week off and really get to know you,' Sherlock offered.

John closed his eyes. The night before he'd sworn he would do anything to move forward with whatever this was, but in the light of day he was all the more aware that they didn't really know each other. They were laying in bed, in one another's arms, and yet they'd hardly progressed beyond the conversation of casual housemates.

'Do you really want that; do you really want me? After last night? Flashbacks won't just go away. I have PTSD and depression. A change of circumstances might help but it won't magically cure those things. Recovery will take me a while, not to mention my physical injuries which may never–'

He stopped when Sherlock kissed him again. 'Do you know what I dream of every night, John?' he asked.

When John didn't answer he went on.

'Falling. Falling not off a roof, but *with* a roof – the entire roof structure of a warehouse sliding sideways off its moorings because someone didn't want to pay to make it safe. And every time I fall it seems to take longer, and I fall further, and I already know just how much it's going to hurt, and there's nothing I can do to stop it. But this time, you saved me,' Sherlock finished with a small smile.

'I saved you?' That didn't seem like the kind of dream a person could be saved from – it was a memory. This was the injury that had led them to meet at the physiotherapist's office, how could John have saved him from something that had already happened?

'I fell but instead of hitting the ground you were there, warm and real and nothing hurt.'

'You mean I stopped you from rolling off the bed,' John laughed at the romance in Sherlock's idea, but it wasn't real.

'In dreams anything is possible,' Sherlock muttered and pressed forward to kiss him again.

The heat of his lips was certainly persuasive.

'Don't confuse your trauma with yourself, John,' Sherlock said against his lips. 'Let me see you, the man who joins a chase he knows nothing about just because I kissed him. The man who does his best to stop a thief because it's the right thing to do.'

Unable to think of anything to say in response, John kissed him back.

The bed was small, but it was soft and Sherlock was warm against his front.

'Okay,' he said. 'A week, to get to know me.'

Present Day – Monkton, North Yorkshire

John roused himself from the daydream when he realised that something had changed about his surroundings. Maybe it hadn't been a daydream. He felt groggy enough that perhaps he'd been asleep.

His face was still pressed against Sherlock's hair.

The fire was still burning brightly.

Sherlock was snoring. Perhaps that's what had woken him.

The moon had risen above the trees now. In the distance beyond the fire and the edge of the campground the river shone like molten mercury, beautiful but unexpectedly treacherous.

A sharp autumn breeze drew up a shower of sparks from the fire and sent a shiver down John's spine.

There was a figure sitting on the other side of the fire.

He stared without moving. Whoever they were, they'd chosen to sit so that the fire was directly between them, which meant that the flames reached high enough to obscure their face.

At last the breeze died down.

'Hello,' he said, as quietly as he could.

Against his shoulder Sherlock slept on, the steady pattern of his snoring continuing without an interruption.

'Hi.' A woman's voice.

'You know, I've never believed in coincidences,' he said in the same low tone, keeping his eyes fixed on the figure but with one ear listening to Sherlock's breathing. 'I've seen them happen, over and over again, and I've dismissed them. I'm a doctor, I use science to save lives or just to make our lives a little more liveable, and, well, coincidences are just not that scientific, are they?'

He laughed a little at the thought of Sherlock trying to quantify coincidence. Whatever method he would choose to test the concept it would certainly involve fire.

'Life has a balance of probabilities, right? The chance of winning the lottery is in the millions but some people win more than once. That's just how chance is.

'When I was ten, I made a new friend,' his voice was turning bitter now. He hated it but he couldn't stop. 'I made a new friend and he turned out to be a missing boy who had been dead for days. Ever since I learned the truth about that I've questioned my sanity every single fucking day. In Afghanistan I saw a girl – a girl who I couldn't resuscitate after she saved her baby sister from a missile strike – standing by the side of the road a week after I watched her family bury her. Less than a minute later a rocket destroyed the ambulance I was travelling in. I'm only here because I believed what I was seeing, even though every fibre of my rational mind says it can't be true.'

The figure on the other side of the fire shook her head and he heard a sound like the first patter of raindrops before a summer storm.

'It sounds like you think about this a lot,' the voice said. She didn't sound all that impressed by the revelation, but then he supposed that *she* wouldn't. 'Don't you want to be alive?'

'I – of course I do.'

He never had those thoughts any more; no matter how dark things got, he never wanted to leave. But he had once, when he was all alone in London with nothing but pain and the memories of the soldiers who'd died around him.

'Good. Being alive is good.'

John thought about the cat. Most of the time he eventually realised when he was seeing someone who had died, but he never said it out loud. Henry had said aloud that Marble was dead; and John had never seen her again.

'You're not alive, though, are you, Gloria?' he asked, half convinced that she'd vanish as the last word left his mouth.

She laughed and it sounded like birds calling out to one another amongst the trees. 'How did you know to find me here?'

'Didn't you hear what I just said about coincidence and probability?'

His relief that she was still there was enough to keep the question from sounding sharp. 'We've been looking for your will. Coming here, camping here, that was a spur of the moment idea.'

He could see her now, or at least he could see the outline of her, backlit by the moon and highlighted by the fire. The river water made her hair hang around her shoulders but with every drop of water that fell from the tight curls it regained a little more of the fullness it had in life. Her eyes danced with the reflected yellow light of the fire and if he concentrated he could see the shine of her lips and the edges of wet clothing.

'I'm glad you found it,' Gloria said with a smile that glittered for an instant before the fire jumped and hid it again. 'I meant to go back to London with the copy and put it somewhere safe. I meant to do a lot of things, when I went home again.'

'You left your luggage at the station. We have your last diary.' He didn't know why it felt important to tell her that, but he felt better for saying it.

She nodded. 'I wasn't up to carrying much any more.'

'By all accounts you saved three children, and possibly a number of anglers. I'd say that's carrying a lot.'

Another smile in the dark.

'I've never talked to someone like you, not–' He searched for a diplomatic wording. 'Not about why you're still here and–'

He was trying to say 'why are you a ghost?' But the phrase was so absurd that he couldn't manage to force it past his lips.

'Why would I leave?' she asked and the fire wavered like someone had passed a gesturing hand through the flames. 'It's beautiful here. I can watch the fish and the birds for hours. I'm not in pain any more. And the water is so dangerous. I can't save everyone, but if I can help even one person then why wouldn't I stay?'

Some part of him wanted to ask if there was anything beyond this but he didn't know if that was something she knew and the rest of him was frightened to find out.

John thought of everything that had brought him to this point, to sitting here with his husband sleeping against his side and he wondered whether it was worth knowing if there was a reason to it all.

The girl in Afghanistan and surviving the roadside attack. Running into Sherlock not once or twice but three times. Hearing his music just when he'd needed it most.

It was almost as if they were meant to be together.

He thought about his health, about all the times he ran around for irregular job assignments, too much stress, too little money; and he didn't see Sherlock all day. He thought about the wedding vows they'd made in a quiet wood-panelled room eight months ago.

Sherlock sighed against his chest, shifted as if he hoped to go back to sleep, then groaned pitifully when he accepted the inevitable and finally sat up.

'Ugh, John, my back is killing me,' he complained while he stretched. 'I had the weirdest dream.'

While Sherlock talked John looked toward the fire again. At first he could swear that he could still see the figure sitting just beyond the flames. But the longer he looked, the more his mind decided her hair was the willow trees near the water and her smile was just the sparks dancing on the wind.

'Let's go to bed,' he said, 'then you can tell me all about it.'

CHAPTER SIXTEEN

Present Day – Monkton, North Yorkshire

IF MR BARRACLOUGH WAS SURPRISED AT THEIR TIRED AND SLIGHTLY unkempt appearance he didn't say anything about it.

A night in borrowed sleeping bags had not been terribly restful so neither of them was feeling at their best, but Sherlock at least was practically vibrating with excitement at the prospect of the will and a possible solution to this whole confusing case.

There was a long, thin envelope sitting between the solicitor's hands.

John was a little bit amazed that Sherlock managed to restrain himself from snatching it up while the man talked.

'My assistant and I were here until 7pm last night looking for this, but we did find it at last,' Mr Barraclough began.

There was a hint of rebuke in his tone, as if it was a scandalously late time of day to still be at work. Given that Sherlock often started new cases in the middle of the night John realised he'd forgotten quite what sensible working hours looked like.

'We appreciate all your hard work.' Sherlock managed to give a sleepy smile that seemed to express the same thing John had just been thinking. After a second he turned his eyes to John and the smile turned into a smirk. Yes, he had been thinking exactly the same thing.

'You said your clients were–' The solicitor paused looking for either his glasses or his notes so Sherlock jumped in with the answer.

'Ian Chilcote, and Jessica Matthews, nee Chilcote.'

The solicitor nodded with a happy smile that made him look ten years younger.

'Well, I absolutely shouldn't be telling you this, Mr Holmes, but my granddaughter showed me all about you on the internet yesterday and I'm sure you can be trusted,' he said gleefully.

'You'd better have your client's solicitor contact me because they're each one-third beneficiaries of Gloria Evans' estate. The third amount goes to a charity in London, assuming that charity is still extant. I do hope so, but if not that amount will go to your clients as well. Given the age of this document there will definitely be some leg work to be done to find up-to-date contact details for some of the organisations listed here, but I believe all the banks at least are still active.'

'What?' Sherlock asked, slightly disbelieving.

'He means 'thank you so much for your help',' John said pleasantly. 'We'll call our clients as soon as we can and have their solicitor get in touch.'

'Do let me know if this turns out to be for a more *interesting* case, Mr Holmes,' Mr Barraclough said, while John nudged the man in question until he shook the hand being offered to him, 'it's been a pleasure working with you.'

'And you!' John added as he hustled Sherlock towards the door.

They'd just got outside when Sherlock said 'What!' again but at twice the volume and with infinitely more indignation.

'Looks like whatever complex scheme they had in mind was entirely unnecessary, then,' John mused, quietly trying to lead Sherlock further away. Perhaps they could make it to the pub, or somewhere with enough signal strength to call a cab to take them back to the city. There was a real bed waiting for them there.

Trying to guide Sherlock didn't work – the skinny detective had suddenly turned to stone.

'They forgot her!' he exclaimed with so much force that John had to wipe spittle from his nose. 'She could have been dead in that flat for years and they never even thought to visit her once! In over thirty years! Instead they invent this bizarre story–'

'Sherlock, you're forgetting that the only address they had wasn't even legible, it took you a whole sheet of paper to decipher it–'

'They should have contacted the dead letter office!'

'I don't think most people know what that is!'

'You saw them, John, you didn't like them any more than I did! Instead of admitting that they hadn't bothered to go looking for her in all this time they came up with this racist, petty–' Sherlock stopped when John put a finger over his lips. His breathing was heavy enough that John was worried about him hyperventilating.

'They were children once. They were children or teenagers when she died,' he said in a slow, reasonable tone. 'She cared about them. Maybe when she stopped visiting they thought that she'd stopped caring. We can show them her books, maybe that will help. And if it doesn't, then…'

He sighed and shrugged. 'It's not our business. We just had to find her. We found her. Now let's go home.'

Sherlock stared at John for a moment then took his hand.

'Okay.'

Present Day – York

A real mattress. Not a musty, borrowed sleeping bag resting one tarpaulin's thickness away from wet grass. A real, soft, double mattress with a thick eiderdown duvet.

John was in heaven.

Well, he was in York, but Sherlock was sleeping soundly beside him so that was close enough.

He snuggled down in the warm comfort of the bed and tried to go back to sleep, but once again the light in the room was wrong.

There was a candle flickering at the end of the bed.

The dead woman was watching him again from beneath the lace of her mob-cap with only vaguely interested eyes. He supposed that made sense; he had ignored her that first night, and if she'd come back on the second he hadn't noticed.

His actions seemed rather rude now.

'Hello,' he said as he sat up, moving carefully to keep Sherlock asleep.

She blinked at him.

'Good evening.' The words came out with effort, like speech had been forgotten long ago and she was surprised she still knew how to do it.

John wondered what that felt like. Gloria was probably the longest dead of anyone he'd ever previously met, most of his other encounters had been after relatively soon after death. Marble the cat had been something of an exception, but he *had* first seen her soon after her death, he'd just kept on seeing her without realising what was going on.

In a way he'd always sort of assumed that dead people appeared because he was there, but Gloria was holding a permanent vigil over that area of the river. What if ghosts were always around? Did they have conversations often? Other than Gloria most didn't seem to know they were dead. Did they just think everyone else was rude?

He realised they were just watching one another in silence.

'Can I help you?' he asked, and then he felt stupid. Had he ever encountered a ghost inside a private residence before? Running into one in the street was one thing, but from her point of view he was inside her house.

She replied with a beckoning gesture.

Well, he had asked.

He climbed stiffly out of bed, his legs still complaining about the previous night at the campground, and shuffled into his slippers before he followed her out of the room. At least he'd gone to bed with clothes on.

In the brighter moonlight of the staircase she became almost invisible, and once or twice he found he could only follow her progress by the glow of her spectral candle.

They were heading for the basement, traditionally the location of a guest house owner's private flat. John was just trying to formulate an excuse for being there – 'I followed a ghost' not generally being an accepted reason for anything at all – when the woman stopped dead, as it were.

She was pointing at a tall cupboard labelled 'storage.'

A thousand possibilities flickered across John's mind – everything from treasure to corpses to evidence of some terrible crime – so when he opened the door to find a vacuum cleaner and a gas waterheater so old that it could have come from the Titanic he was a little disappointed.

Disappointed and a little dizzy. He peered into the darkness of the cupboard, noting the thick soot stains on the wall but unable to see much else since the only light was from a ghostly candle and the yellow of the boiler's pilot light.

Gas pilot lights were supposed to be blue.

'Mr Watson? Are you lost?' the landlady asked from directly behind him, making him jump.

'It's Doctor, actually,' he said as he turned to face her. His ghostly companion was nowhere to be seen. He could feel a headache creeping in at the edges of his awareness.

'Why are you in the storage cupboard at two in the morning?'

He smiled reassuringly at her and completely ignored the question. 'Do you have a carbon monoxide detector?' he asked instead.

Her expression switched instantly from confused to worried at his tone of voice. He'd always been good at getting patients' attention.

'Yes, in the kitchen downstairs, why?'

'Do you suffer from headaches at all? Nausea?'

She nodded. 'Sometimes, but I thought it was just my age. Should I go get that detector?'

'Please.'

The device started beeping before she'd reached the top of the staircase again.

'What do I do?' she asked, wild-eyed.

John rubbed at his forehead, trying to remember the carbon monoxide poisoning advice he'd seen online, but as she was turning the detector nervously in her hands she noticed a sticker on the back.

'Oh. It says here I should turn everything off, open the windows and call an engineer. Do you think I should do that?'

'Yes,' John said. 'Yes, I do. I'm going to go back to my room now and get out of your hair while you deal with this, but I'll open the windows on the stairs for you on my way up. Okay?'

She was already bustling away in the direction of the phone but as she disappeared around the corner of the stairs again she said, 'Oh, yes, thank you, Doctor Watson, you're a life saver.'

John didn't stop again until he was on the top floor of the house, where he sat on the bomb-damaged windowsill that had been pointed out during their first visit and opened the window wide. The breeze soon cleared his head, and the quiet sounds of the nighttime street below were restful.

There was still no sign of the woman with the candle.

Perhaps it was enough for her to keep the residents of the house safe.

Maybe it was time he started paying better attention.

He returned to bed when a colourful van with 'Emergency 24 Hour Assistance' painted down the side pulled up in front of the guest house. The sun had yet to make an appearance on the horizon and the city was still sleeping.

Sherlock grumbled in his sleep when John opened the window in their room, but he soon quieted again once he was in firmly wrapped in John's arms.

John woke the next morning unsure whether his encounter in the night had just been a dream, but feeling better rested than he had in months.

Outside it was the middle of the day, bright sunshine streamed in through the open window, and they were going to spend the rest of the day in bed just because they could.

He watched through half-open eyes as Sherlock turned another page of the book in his hand. It was one of Gloria's diaries, one of the older ones, written before her health declined. Sherlock handled it delicately, turning every page with care, but he moved quickly through the contents at a speed that John had once found unbelievable. Now he just found it cute.

'Did I tell you that I dreamed you met Gloria?' Sherlock asked suddenly. 'At the campsite.'

'Yes, you told me when you woke up,' John said through a yawn that was only slightly affected. This was a topic he wanted to make boring.

Sherlock continued but didn't look away from the book. 'You were just talking to her across the fire like it was no surprise that a dead woman was making social calls.'

'Huh.'

'It was strange.'

John hummed in agreement but when Sherlock didn't provide any more details John took the opportunity to change the subject.

'While you were sleeping on me out there I did some thinking,' he began. 'About us, and work.'

'Is this one of those conversations where I need to put the book down and concentrate fully, or is it more of a 'yes, dear' conversation?' Sherlock asked.

Fortunately, his tone and raised eyebrow made it clear he was joking as he placed Gloria's diary carefully onto the bedside table and rolled over so that they were facing one another.

John glowered at him anyway.

That just made Sherlock kiss him, which would only lead to more kisses. So, John stroked his hand through Sherlock's hair and gently urged him back.

'Behave.'

Sherlock grumbled but he did as he was told, his own hand drifting up to trace the shell of John's ear.

'Thank you,' John said, then he realised how solemn he sounded and laughed. 'Sorry, I just want to talk seriously about this for a while. I can't keep taking any agency job I can get. I don't want us to be always missing each other because the schedule changes every single day. I can't keep on running around London after you then going back out a few hours later for the twelve-hour shift.

'I'm going to look for a practice that I can join on a part-time basis. Maybe one that works with combat veterans in particular. Not a lot of hours. Enough to keep my hand in and training up to date so if I have to support us full time I can. Two, or two-and-a-half days a week. It won't be flexible but the rest of the time I can work with you if you need me.'

'Or – you could rest,' Sherlock said. He stroked John's ear again in a gentle gesture that was just this side of ticklish.

'That, too.'

'And you'll get your health checked out as soon as we get home.'

'I promise.'

'Good.' Sherlock grinned. He leaned forward against John's grip and kissed him.

Much to his disappointment just as John started to kiss back, Sherlock pulled away.

'Ears!'

'What?' It was a futile question but John asked it anyway.

'We didn't call the clients yet, did we?' Sherlock asked, leaping out of the bed to begin pawing through one of the suitcases.

'No, Sherlock,' John said slowly, 'we were going to call them after dinner, the reception is terrible in here. Remember?'

'Good, we need to call Lestrade, the clients aren't the clients!'

John asked 'What?' again even though he knew it wouldn't help.

'Ears, John! Ears!'

'Yes, Sherlock, everyone has them…'

Sherlock stood up, and pointed at him. 'Exactly, but they don't change, do they?'

John had to think about that for a moment while Sherlock arranged a number of Gloria's diaries across the duvet. He wasn't exactly a specialist in ears but he'd certainly read somewhere that they didn't change much after birth. Hadn't Sherlock once mentioned someone being convicted on the basis of an ear print?

'Look at these,' Sherlock said. He'd climbed onto John's side of the bed so they could look at the laid-out images together.

Half a dozen of Gloria's sketches of the children 'I & J' laid out side by side. She was a skilled amateur and seemed to prefer to draw profiles.

'All the ears are consistent for both children,' John said after studying them all. He wasn't sure if that was the right answer. He'd never really looked at ears in that much detail before.

Sherlock offered John his phone.

'Okay, now look at this security photo from the flat.'

'You have a camera in our flat?' That was one of John's own personal nightmares; wherever Sherlock put it there would be incriminating footage.

'Calm down, it's only on the stairs,' Sherlock said in his least-sincere voice as he offered up the phone again.

John took it and the difference was obvious. John had been expecting some tiny detail in the curve of the pinna or the shape of a helix, but where the children in the sketches had detached lobes the clients' lobes were very obviously attached.

'You're right, they're completely different!'

'Exactly! I think that's why their scheme made no sense; they had no background information. They probably found the documents or some letter got misdirected to them and they thought they could take advantage. I need to ring Lestrade!'

Sherlock reached for his phone but John caught his wrist.

'No, wait, I have a better idea.'

'Yeah?'

'Get dressed,' John said with a grin, 'we're going back to London and we'll present all of this to the police ourselves.'

Sherlock kissed him so hard that John's lips stung at the pressure.

It felt like he was trying to pour all his gratitude into the gesture but it just made it harder for John to resist the urge to pull him back into bed. He had to push Sherlock away and towards their suitcases.

The kiss broken, Sherlock went willingly, though he flashed John one more smile as he grabbed his jeans. 'I love you.'

'I love you too, but you still owe me a real holiday.'

Improbable
PRESS

THE AUTHOR

G.V. PEARCE

G.V. is a mysterious being said to haunt the North York Moors, but is otherwise as yet unclassified by science.

Rumour has it that they can be summoned by leaving coffee in a faery circle at midnight.

Also from Improbable Press

 AN IMPRINT OF CLAN DESTINE PRESS AUSTRALIA

www.improbablepress.com

THE CASE OF THE MISPLACED MODELS

BY TESSA BARDING

Dr Watson arrives at his surgery one morning to find a stranger about to staple his own leg injury together. Days later, John Watson coincidentally accepts a flatshare with the same man; and before long is laughing, running, and falling in love with the endlessly-fascinating Sherlock Holmes.

While the 'consulting detective' barely seems to notice John, he does agree to help when they learn of the sudden and curious death of John's friend Karim Halabi.

Karim was acidentally shot during a game of laser tag. Case closed, say the police. But as John and Sherlock dig deeper it seems that Karim's death was no accident. It also becomes clear to John that Sherlock's feelings for him are much deeper too.

A QUESTION OF TIME

BY JAMIE ASHBIRD

Sherlock Holmes – whether he's a student in 1980, a consulting detective in 47 BCE, or a smitten neighbour in 1969 – will always find his

John Watson – whether he is a military doctor in 1917, an angry Saxon with an axe in 1086, or a priest in 1603.

A Question of Time is an illustrated journey through the ages told by our heroes, by their friends, by a scorched manuscript...

And in precisely 221 words; with the last one starting with B.

A Study in Velvet and Leather

by K. Caine

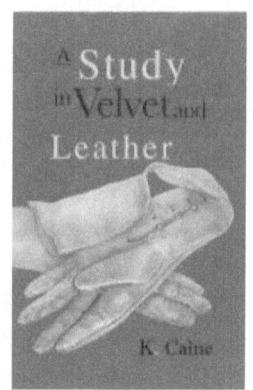

Sharing a flat with Sherlock Holmes should not have posed a problem for John Watson – after all, Watson is gay, Holmes is a woman, and the arrangement is financially convenient.

But when Holmes takes on a complex case involving Irene Adler and a scandalous photo, she turns to Watson for assistance.

The case leads them everywhere from the opera to a secret Victorian BDSM club, and Watson soon finds himself questioning his partnership with Holmes, his sexuality, and his understanding of himself.

The Adventure of the Colonial Boy

by Narrelle M Harris

It's 1893, and Dr John Watson, still mourning his friend after his death at the Reichenbach Falls, is now triply bereaved by his wife Mary's death in childbirth. Then a telegram from Australia interrupts his grief: *Come at once if convenient.*

Desperate to believe Holmes may still be alive, Watson takes an unexpectedly dangerous voyage to the Australian colony of Victoria.

And soon Holmes and Watson are racing through bohemian Melbourne, tackling a series of murders linked to a red leech and a remnant of Moriarty's gang. But things are not as they were.

Can Sherlock Holmes and Dr Watson solve a crime, save a life, rediscover trust...and admit to love?

A DREAM TO BUILD A KISS ON

BY NARRELLE M HARRIS

John Watson, invalided army doctor, part-time artist, and Sherlock Holmes, consulting detective, become flatmates and friends in contemporary London.

Love grows too, despite past betrayals and present dangers – for where you have Holmes and Watson, there too are Moriarty and Moran.

A Dream to Build a Kiss On explores love and family, trust and betrayal, forgiveness and revenge, brothers and brothers-in-arms.

It's an ongoing tale, told in chapters of 221 words – with the last one starting with B.

A MURMURING OF BEES

EDITED BY ATLIN MERRICK

Think of Sherlock Holmes and you think of mysteries, John Watson, and bees.

Here bees are front and centre in tales of secret diaries, rare nectars, and the private language of lovers, where John and Sherlock are helping each other, romancing each other, *loving* each other.

Contributors:

Amy L Webb, Anarion, Atlin Merrick, Brittany Russ, Darcy Lindbergh, Elinor Gray, Hallie Deighton, Jamie Ashbird, Janet A-Nunn, Kerry Greenwood, Kim Le Patourel, Kimber Camacho, Lucy Jarsdell, Meredith Spies, Morgan Black, Narrelle M. Harris, Poppy Alexander, Stacey Albright, Tessa Barding, Verena, Verity Burns.

Sherlock Holmes and John Watson:
The Night They Met

by Atlin Merrick

Some things belong together, the one with the other, natural pairs.

Sherlock Holmes and John Watson.

Whether it's in an empty house during the Blitz, a West London strip club in the 70s, or deep in the heart of a Hong Kong computer lab, the meeting of these two legendary men is inevitable.

Spanning 128 years, here are 19 stories of that destiny: of how, no matter where they are or when, a detective meets a doctor; of how they change each other in heart and mind; of how they fall in love.

Sherlock Holmes and John Watson:
The Day They Met

by Atlin Merrick

Fifty new ways the world's most legendary friendship might have begun...

Sherlock Holmes and John Watson have wandered far from the light of Victorian gas lamps. As Holmes and Watson they've tangled with Nazis, as Sherlock and John they roam the corridors of New Scotland Yard.

In a world of so many fresh adventures, why not fresh beginnings to those adventures?

From an 1879 Kabul train station to a King's College lecture theatre in 2015, *The Day They Met* includes stories both classic and contemporary, offering fifty intriguing new ways that the world's most legendary partnership might have begun.